Haunted House

Also From Heather Graham

Slow Burn
Night Heat

From 1001 Dark Nights
Blood Night
Hallow Be The Haunt
Crimson Twilight
When Irish Eyes Are Haunting
All Hallow's Eve
Blood on the Bayou
Haunted Be the Holidays
The Dead Heat of Summer

Haunted House

A Krewe of Hunters Novella

By Heather Graham

1001 DARK NIGHTS

PRESS

Haunted House
A Krewe of Hunters Novella
Copyright 2021 Heather Graham Pozzessere
ISBN: 978-1-951812-70-6

Foreword: Copyright 2014 M. J. Rose

Published by 1001 Dark Nights Press, an imprint of Evil Eye Concepts, Incorporated

Sign up for the 1001 Dark Nights Newsletter
and be entered to win a Tiffany Key necklace.

There's a contest every month!

Go to www.1001DarkNights.com to subcribe.

**As a bonus, all subscribers can download
FIVE FREE exclusive books!**

One Thousand and One Dark Nights

Once upon a time, in the future...

*I was a student fascinated with stories and learning.
I studied philosophy, poetry, history, the occult, and
the art and science of love and magic. I had a vast
library at my father's home and collected thousands
of volumes of fantastic tales.*

*I learned all about ancient races and bygone
times. About myths and legends and dreams of all
people through the millennium. And the more I read
the stronger my imagination grew until I discovered
that I was able to travel into the stories... to actually
become part of them.*

*I wish I could say that I listened to my teacher
and respected my gift, as I ought to have. If I had, I
would not be telling you this tale now.
But I was foolhardy and confused, showing off
with bravery.*

*One afternoon, curious about the myth of the
Arabian Nights, I traveled back to ancient Persia to
see for myself if it was true that every day Shahryar
(Persian: شهريار, "king") married a new virgin, and then
sent yesterday's wife to be beheaded. It was written
and I had read that by the time he met Scheherazade,
the vizier's daughter, he'd killed one thousand
women.*

*Something went wrong with my efforts. I arrived
in the midst of the story and somehow exchanged
places with Scheherazade – a phenomena that had
never occurred before and that still to this day, I
cannot explain.*

*Now I am trapped in that ancient past. I have
taken on Scheherazade's life and the only way I can
protect myself and stay alive is to do what she did to
protect herself and stay alive.*

*Every night the King calls for me and listens as I spin tales.
And when the evening ends and dawn breaks, I stop at a
point that leaves him breathless and yearning for more.
And so the King spares my life for one more day, so that
he might hear the rest of my dark tale.*

*As soon as I finish a story... I begin a new
one... like the one that you, dear reader, have before
you now.*

Chapter 1

The thing seemed to stare at her.

Of course, it couldn't stare. There was nothing but stygian emptiness where the eyes should have been. The soft tissue had long ago decomposed. And still...

She knew she was in Salem, Massachusetts, renowned for tragic history and ghost stories. And it was almost Halloween. October. *Haunted Happenings* was coming into full swing, filled with scary fun and delight and...

This.

Dear Lord, it was something straight out of a horror movie. Except that...

It was real!

She was dreaming. Somehow, Kylie Connelly Dickson knew she was dreaming. She also knew that, somehow, the dream was real.

And she knew where she was and what was going on—as if she had entered the very soul of another human being.

She was in an old house. One known for its tragic history, curses, hauntings, and all that came with such a place.

Once, Kylie hadn't understood. Now, since she'd met Jon, she knew something about her unique talent—enough to know that she was seeing, feeling, and *knowing* things as another person.

And she knew the circumstances because she had the memories and information of the soul she had entered.

She *was* another person at the moment.

She even knew who she was this time...her friend, Brenda Riley.

And she knew that she had just purchased the home. She knew what Brenda did because, in a very strange way, she *was* Brenda. She saw with her eyes, felt her emotions. Knew her thoughts.

Which told her that the electricity wouldn't be on until later. Unfortunately, the realtor handling the sale hadn't thought she'd be able to get into the home until tomorrow. But, as it turned out, she had signed the last papers today.

It had been a lifelong dream to buy the amazingly historic home in the city she loved so very much. Mandy Nichols, the realtor for the absentee seller, had been wonderful, hurrying things along as best she could, knowing how much Brenda loved the house.

But this...

She was amazed that she hadn't screamed. Maybe because—in the Halloween season—all kinds of pranks and shenanigans went on. Or perhaps, more likely, it was because all her breath was gone, and she had nearly passed out. And though her flashlight reflected off the white gleam of the skull and other skeletal remains stuffed behind the deteriorating false wall, she still hadn't moved.

Because she was frozen stiff with shock and fear.

The house that had stood before had belonged to a woman accused of witchcraft. Not one who had been executed, but one who had died, nonetheless. Her family had left Salem, cursing the very ground. Sometime after their marriage, it was said that Ezekiel Johnson murdered his wife. And in the 1800s, Priscilla Alcott had, in turn, murdered her husband. And then, in the 1900s, Fisher Smith had been accused by the locals of being a serial killer after citizens of Salem, Peabody, and other nearby towns disappeared. Even in 2001, a ghost tour guide had vanished after pointing out the house, the ghosts of the dead who haunted it, and stating how the land itself had been cursed.

But this...

It had to be a prank.

A prank, a prank, a prank...

But it wasn't. She had just leaned against the wall, and it had proven to be false with perhaps two feet behind it. And there, shoved against the old brick and structural beams held up by the jagged structure of the real wall, was the skeleton.

People had warned her. Most of them would be laughing as they considered the tales of the Brim House to be nothing but urban legends created with the use of a wee bit of history. A woman had died in the original home that had stood here during the infamous witch trials. She hadn't been executed, but she had suffered so seriously from malnutrition and disease while being held in the crowded jail that she had just made it home after her relatives painfully scraped together the money to pay her jail fees, only to die shortly after.

Then, there had been the murder. A family member, luring an old enemy to the house...

So many tales.

Some true. Some purely fabricated.

Well, this—this skull and these bones—they were old. *Very old*, she thought. Because it was all held together with jagged brick and the remnants of whatever the person had been wearing. She couldn't even tell if they had been male or female—not even in the strange glaring light and shadow of the flashlight.

She played the light beyond the eerie skull and bone and rotting bits of fabric on the thing and showed that *more* lay behind it, buried behind what no one had apparently known was a false wall.

The beams were old, lines of time etched into them. Perhaps old building markers, splinters of wood jaggedly sticking here and there on...no. Please, no.

More? Dear God, she could see...flesh.

She wasn't about to look any further.

She found her voice and willed the paralysis of her fear to subside. With a terrified squeal, she turned and fled out of the den, hurried through the parlor, and rushed out of the front door to the colonial-style porch. She didn't stop there, but she didn't go to her car parked in the drive, either.

Mr. Flannery, her neighbor to the left, was clipping a rose from a bush. He was an older gentleman, and from what she had seen, he was still tender to his wife. The rose was likely for her. He lifted a hand to Brenda in a cheerful wave.

With a jerk, she returned the gesture. She tried to smile but couldn't. He and Mrs. Flannery were all into it being October. Their yard held a gruesome, grinning demon. And several strange, lighted creatures with wild and crazy faces decorated the porch columns and all the bushes around the place.

That was it, surely...

Halloween. Her house. Someone had gotten in ahead of her. She was being pranked! The neighbors, maybe? Though it was a strange way to welcome her to the neighborhood.

Except, deep down, she knew that wasn't the case.

And she needed to move. But she was still so shocked.

Ginger Radisson and her boyfriend Kenny stepped out of the house to the right of her new purchase. She'd met them while engaged in negotiations to buy Brim House. Nice people. Kenny was there most of the time.

They smiled and waved.

"Getting into the house, Brenda?" Ginger called to her.

She was afraid she wouldn't be able to speak.

What if they had done it? What if her normal-looking neighbors were homicidal maniacs?

"I just stopped by," she managed to call out. "Tomorrow—electricity!"

Kenny had gone all out in their yard for the holiday, too. Skeletons dangled from the two oak trees near the road. Jack-o'-lanterns had been strewn up the path to the porch. No witches flew about the yard, though—other neighbors were Wiccan, and she figured Ginger and Kenny were sensitive to the fact that the images might be offensive to them.

The couple got into Kenny's little red sedan and moved on.

Down the street, she saw a man in his late teens or early twenties walking a medium-sized dog—a mutt, though a mix of *what* she didn't know. The young man was the friendly type, too. He waved. She managed to wave back. Still frightened, she stayed glued to the sidewalk. She thought he might be Calvin Daily, the adult son of the Daily family, here to watch the house and the family pup while his parents visited his sister at college in California. The people here were friendly. Mr. Flannery had told her about her other neighbors and about many of the people living on the street.

But now…

Now, she found herself imagining that they were evil, like the tall fellow walking from one house down the block to another. A family named Matheson lived on the left. This was probably the dad.

She was letting herself panic and behave crazily and irrationally.

But she wasn't going back inside the house.

She ran toward the main street ahead, the city green, the hotel that had been there almost forever, and the shops, restaurants, and life around it.

No, no, no…get a grip!

It was October. *Haunted Happenings* was in full swing.

Only when she was close to some semblance of teeming humanity, where surely dozens of people could not be evil, did she stop. Locals were still out and about or working, lots of tourists… She didn't know everyone who lived in Salem, but she *did* know a lot of the staff at several of the restaurants. She knew many of the people giving their initial speeches to tourists flocked around them for ghost tours. And yet…

Haunted Happenings. The town was filled to the gills with everything creepy and…

Evil.

Still, she was around people. Lots and lots of them.

Living folks who did not live on her street.

All she could do was stand there, trying not to shake. Attempting to convince herself that she was a normal and rational human being. She was an adult—a young woman who had grown up in this town. And Salem was old—hundreds of years old—and the skeleton in her wall…it had been there for a long, long time.

But something was behind it. Something that had once been…alive.

And not that long ago.

She was on a corner. She could turn back and see the house. Find out if it had come to life, or if a demon glow surrounded it, something that betrayed the fact that it was cursed as the family who had lived there had once been.

Night had come, and the moon was high. A ground fog swirled in a soft gray mist. Caught in the silver mist and moonlight, the place did indeed look like a haunted house.

I don't believe in haunted houses, she reminded herself. She had led ghost tours and had lived with the sad history of Salem all her life. There was good history, too, though. Change had happened because of the tragedy in the area. And throughout the hundreds of years, new generations had come and gone. The country had seen a revolution, a civil war, two world wars, and more. Whaling and seafaring had been big. Fishing was still a commercial venture. Now bankers, accountants, and people with so-called normal jobs lived and worked and raised their children here.

But…

She checked her watch. She hadn't realized it had grown so late. Well, in the grand scheme of a night crowd, it wasn't *that* late, but even in late summer, the light was gone from the northern sky by eight forty-five. She'd meant to leave work early while it was still light, knowing full well that she didn't have electricity in the house yet. But when it had grown late, she hadn't cared. The papers were all signed. The house was hers. She actually owned it. Of course, there was still a lot of work to be done because the place had grown truly derelict, but before the sale, the absentee owners had seen to it that the kitchen had been updated, and there was one bedroom she could use immediately.

No way in hell was she sleeping in a house with a skeleton hidden in a false wall, though. All she had done was lean against it in the dark. She had broken through, and then…

She took a breath. *Calm down.* Whatever had happened to the poor being in the wall had happened long ago. As to what lay behind it…

Maybe her imagination had taken flight. It *was* Halloween. People went creepy-crazy at Halloween. But…

She knew. She just *knew*. The skeleton was no prank. It was real. No matter what lay behind it.

Nope. She wasn't sleeping in the house. She needed the workers to come in, but it was Thursday, and they weren't due until Saturday.

Call somebody, she told herself. The police…

What would the authorities do about a body that had obviously been there a very long time?

Still, she had to call *someone*. Maybe somebody at the Peabody Essex Museum. Maybe—

A scream rose within her. A skeleton, even one maybe hundreds of years old, was one thing.

But what lay behind it…

The world suddenly seemed to be made of mist and haze. First, she felt a strange sense of withdrawal, and then she was no longer seeing through the eyes of another person. She was no longer in the body and soul of another—someone she knew. Her friend, Brenda Riley.

"Kylie!"

Kylie woke with a start, blinking as the images of Salem faded completely into the mist, and that sensation of *being* someone else disappeared altogether.

She didn't know if she had screamed. She just instantly knew where she was—at home in Alexandria, Virginia, in the little townhouse she and Jon Dickson had purchased right before they got married.

And Jon was there. That made the world seem sane again. She was herself once more, and she was okay.

Because Jon was there, touching her, holding her, his deep blue eyes filled with concern, his dark hair tousled because…

Well, they *were* still considered newlyweds. They'd eaten the subs they'd picked up for dinner, and some silly thing had gotten them going. They'd headed up to the bedroom, clothing strewn all along the way. They'd laughed, grown passionate, teased and made love, and then…

They'd drifted off to sleep.

And in her sleep, that strange thing that happened to Kylie—the gift or curse of being in another person's skin—had taken hold of her again.

"Kylie? What happened? Where were you?" Jon asked, pulling her to him and holding her gently against him.

She groaned softly. "I was…with Brenda. My friend from Salem. I was her for a few minutes there, Jon."

It had happened to her before. But that had been with friends at a bachelorette party under a past life regression. She had seen herself as someone else, being murdered.

That was when she'd met Jon. He'd been on the trail of a serial killer. She'd nearly passed out in a pub, and they'd…

He'd believed her. And he'd found her some help. They'd had a bit of a rough go of it at first, but the case he'd been on had been strange and intense, and the resolution even stranger. But he'd given her the ability to recognize the fact that she wasn't crazy—just part of humanity with a few extra rare and unusual senses. And she had been attracted to him from the beginning. So, they'd worked together, and from there…

She gave herself a mental shake.

"There are bodies in Brenda's house," she said, wincing. "I was…there. It sounds so horrible, but I was there, like before. I was her—or inside her, anyway. I knew what she knew and felt and saw what she did. She came in with her flashlight, so excited to finally have the house. She'd bought the place and signed the papers early and had just come in. It was dark, and she was in the den. She leaned against the wall and…it gave."

"Is Brenda all right?" Jon asked. "Are *you* all right?" he added softly.

"Brenda is physically fine, just terrified. As for me…I think so," Kylie said, just as her phone rang. Jon leaned back, and she reached past him for the bedside table to answer the call. He watched her, frowning as she did.

"It's going to be Brenda," he said.

And he was right.

Kylie had barely said, "Hello," before Brenda started talking.

"Oh, Kylie, thank God you answered. I don't know what to do. But you know Salem, and you know Brim House. I know you're not from here, but you are from Massachusetts, and you've been here often. I mean, it was cool that we met at that party when we were both here from our different colleges on break. Not that that really makes any difference. But you loved history like I love history, and you have always known so much about the past happenings here and…"

"Brenda, what's going on?"

"I bought Brim House. I've always wanted the place. It's sat empty for so long, and it's so rich in history and, okay, rumor, but now… Oh, Kylie."

"What happened?" Kylie asked, looking at Jon. He was staring at her, listening. Then he reached for his phone, rolled off the bed, and stood to make a call.

Brenda continued.

"I'm sorry to call you like this, but you're married to a man in the FBI. *You're* not FBI, but I know you helped him during that murder investigation here in Salem. I didn't know who else to call. I don't know what to do. And I know your husband is Special Agent Dickson—I mean, obviously. I was on vacation in London when you guys were here before, but I heard all about what happened. And I did get to meet Jon at the wedding. Well…maybe he won't mind if I just ask him what to do?" Brenda said, rambling and obviously frightened.

"He would never mind you asking him for help, Brenda—" Kylie began.

But Brenda was a pile of nerves. She seemed not to have heard Kylie as she rushed on.

"They're true, Kylie. Some of the stories about Brim House must be true. I mean, that it's haunted and that murders happened here. Today was my first day as the new owner, and I *had* to go in. And, Kylie, the dead are in my house. They're in my walls. Please, please, can you come up? And quickly? I am so, so scared."

Kylie looked over at Jon.

A moment of fear filled her again.

Salem. She had loved Salem all her life.

But she'd nearly been killed there.

And this…

Resolve filled her as she looked at her husband. He had given her the strength to accept her strange fifth sense—and what might well be a sixth sense, too. He had given her so much more than that, as well. He was solid. His sense of justice was great. His will was strong. And his care for others—his desire to seek the truth and end evil before it could claim more victims—was something that drew her to him.

She'd gained so much from him: her acceptance of her strangeness and the courage to move forward and think even when terrified.

Looking at him now, she knew.

Yes, they were going to Salem.

Chapter 2

Jon Dickson felt a sense of dread.

Brenda lived in Salem, Massachusetts. And while he loved the city—he'd been born and had grown up there—the concept of a friend calling Kylie for help after she'd done one of her strange in-body visits was alarming.

And sad.

Because it had started off as such a great night. He'd just wrapped up a case with his fellow agents—one that had gone well. A twelve-year-old had disappeared on his way home from baseball practice. Thanks to a friend—the kind only the Krewe could usually see—they had tracked down the kidnapper in record time, stopping what might have been a ransom situation—or far worse.

Jon had had an early night, and Kylie had gotten home early, as well, happy because her fellow docent at the Washington, D.C. Museum of History, was working out wonderfully.

Jon seldom had early days since field agents often tended to work into the night—something the agents in the Krewe of Hunters accepted. They were also, by nature, willing to accommodate each other when needed.

Kylie's hours were better. She was a researcher and docent—beloved by Adam Harrison their philanthropist founder, who had funded the museum—and she was incredibly happy with her work, lecturing for other venues sometimes, but usually home by six or seven. The museum had variable hours.

Today had been special. They'd both been home by four.

And they'd found themselves ordering in and had headed up to bed early—hey, they were still newlyweds! A great deal of delightful activity later, and they had dozed off…

Until Kylie's dream. Or vision. Or whatever it was that her subconscious did when she entered another person's being and saw through their eyes. He woke, immediately worried that she seemed to be in such a distressed and restless state.

Hearing Brenda on the phone, and knowing Kylie's dream forbode something bad, he put through a call to Jackson Crow.

Luckily, his field supervisor was accustomed to calls at all hours of the day and night. They spoke quickly, and he said he would give Jackson more details when he knew them.

Jon just knew they'd be heading for Salem.

As he finished his call, he heard Brenda's nervous and excited voice through Kylie's cell, even though the phone wasn't on speaker. He couldn't quite make out the words, though. Kylie had met Brenda in college and had gone to see her time and again during Kylie's many trips to Salem throughout the years, so it made sense that she would reach out.

"Brenda, calm down, please—" Kylie tried.

Kylie looked at Jon, shaking her head and frowning slightly.

Jon and Kylie had been together for more than a year now, and had been man and wife for several months of that time.

He still loved just watching her, seeing her, taking in the soft fall of her auburn hair, the light in her eyes—green and brown and sometimes a bit gold. Her face had been crafted with elegant features, and yet that wasn't what created the depth of beauty in her. Kylie *cared*. She cared for others around her. Jon never had to explain a late night at work or his worry about a friend or even a stranger.

"Wait, wait, Brenda. Wait, hold on."

Kylie placed the call on mute and looked at him, shaking her head. "Okay, so Brenda got her new house—"

"Right. I remember you mentioning one night that Brenda desperately wanted to buy one of the historic houses," he said. "So—"

"There really are dead bodies in her wall."

"What?"

"She's standing out on the street right now, down the block from her new place. She went there after work and leaned against a wall in the den. Apparently, the drywall gave because it's a false wall, and she found a skeleton in the space behind it. And then…"

"That's what you saw through Brenda's eyes earlier?"

Kylie nodded. "She thinks there's a newer body."

"You were there," he said softly. "What do *you* think?"

Kylie winced and nodded.

"Okay," Jon said quietly. "Kylie, I'm happy to go to Salem and help Brenda, but if she has bodies in her walls and is standing in the street, she needs help faster than we can give it to her. It's a seven-hour drive. Even if I ask for my unit's jet, it might still be several hours before we can get to her. Tell her I'll call a detective. A good guy, a friend—"

"Ben Miller?" Kylie asked.

He nodded. Kylie had met Ben during the case that had brought the two of them together.

"We'll be there as soon as possible. I just called Jackson, and he cleared me already to go for as long as we need. What about you? Sometimes, I think you *are* the information desk for the museum."

"The new guy is great. And Adam loves him. I'm in good shape."

Jon reached over and glanced at Kylie. "May I?" he asked her.

Kylie handed him the phone.

"Brenda, it's Jon. We're going to come up. But you need help sooner than we can get there—it's a bit of a drive from northern Virginia. But I have a friend there—great guy—a local detective named Ben Miller. I'm going to call him, and I know he'll get to you as soon as possible. For now, just head over to the Hawthorne and wait for him at the bar. It doesn't sound as if you want to be alone."

"Alone, no. I don't want to be alone. I mean, I may not know anyone at the bar, but you're right, there will be people and…um, your friend… Should I have just called 911? Or…Jon, I don't know when that false wall went up. It's decaying, so I guess it's been a while, but…I think there's a body *behind* the skeleton that's being held together by bits of clothing or…maybe the wall itself. I mean, the skeleton is held by the wall or…I don't know. But I think I saw flesh. I don't know how long it takes for a body to decompose—"

"Brenda, I'm going to call the detective right now. Go to the hotel like I said." He paused. "No one who might still be alive and in danger is in the wall, right? Ben will get a medical examiner out there to make sure, but… Did you lock the house?" Jon asked her.

Kylie shook her head.

Brenda voiced a, "No."

"All right. Wait for Ben. And stay around people."

"It doesn't have anything to do with me, right? I mean, it was just a good place to—to dispose of a body, right?" Brenda asked him weakly.

"If you're out of your apartment—"

"Oh, I still have it tonight. But I think I'll stay at the hotel as you suggested. I just wish—I'm so afraid to be alone."

"We'll be there as soon as we can. We can probably start driving in about fifteen minutes. And, thankfully, at this hour, traffic around the Capitol shouldn't be too bad."

"Oh, thank you. Thank you so much," Brenda said. "All right, I'm going. I'm already walking over to the hotel."

Jon handed the phone back to Kylie, making another call himself.

Ben Miller answered with a groan.

"Thanks, I feel so appreciated," Jon said, certain Ben knew it was him—he'd likely have glanced at his caller I.D.

"Sorry. But if you're calling me, although it may be good for me or us in a way I can't quite fathom, I don't see you calling me at this hour to tell me anything *good*. I'm guessing you need my help on something. And, actually, I could use yours."

"Why? What's happened?"

"You know this place. You're from here."

"Yes," Jon said carefully. He was surprised to feel defensive. Sure, Salem was practically immersed in the past and in its unique place that it held in the history of the nation. But it was also a nice place where people lived and worked and raised their children.

While it was true that the city had gone commercial, making money off tourism in all its guises, it also led to more legends.

More ghosts.

And, sometimes, depraved people decided it was a good place to carry out their crimes.

"Two tourists went missing." Ben hesitated for a minute. "Halloween," he said mournfully. "We watched, were alert—and a crazy perp still slipped through. Jon, I'm sure you heard about the murderer who strung up his victim like a scarecrow, right? Through the years and across the country, people know that others will open their doors for trick-or-treaters. They know children and teens will be out walking the streets, and that adults will be going to parties or events and coming home from them—intoxicated, a lot of the time. And people are dressed up in costumes. Even on video, it's hard to identify a clown with face paint, a bulging nose and a giant red wig."

Ben was on a rant, but his words were true. Delightful fun for the many could easily become an opportunity for the hunter.

"So...something like that already happened?" Jon asked.

Ben let out a long breath. "We found a victim. Forty-year-old woman from Utah. Someone hid her inside one of the giant jack-o'-lanterns that forms the border for an outdoor theater." Ben was quiet for a minute. "They dosed her with a massive dose of rat poison and left her there sometime between performances. We've been looking for the second woman. Checking every ridiculous Halloween decoration out there."

Jon lowered his head and closed his eyes for a minute.

"I may know where your second victim is," he said quietly. He explained what Kylie's friend had just called about.

"Brim House? I heard it just sold," Ben said. "And that place...well, the stories abound. Is she frightened? How has no one seen this corpse or body or remains before? Do you think someone thought they were being funny and decided to play a cruel Halloween trick on her?"

"I have no idea." Jon hesitated for a minute. He couldn't explain Kylie's unusual talent to Ben. But if Kylie had entered Brenda's consciousness, then something was very wrong. "Ben, I want you to find out what's going on. Kylie and I are on our way, but it will take us several hours to drive up. The door to the place is open. If you can get a medical examiner in there, please, Ben, get started on whatever is going on right away. Oh, and could you stop by the Hawthorne and tell Brenda that she can hang at the police station or something? She's absolutely terrified. We can text you a picture of her so you know what to look for. We told her to wait at the bar."

"I'll get right on it," Ben promised. "And you're driving?"

"We can leave right now and we won't have to deal with getting a car from Boston or a private airfield. I don't think getting a plane will be any faster anyway. Keep in touch, will you?"

"You got it."

Jon ended the call and looked at Kylie.

She had ended her call with Brenda, too.

"All right. We need to go."

She smiled weakly at him.

"Maybe we should put on some clothes first."

"Probably, except...damn. The night started out so good."

She stood and walked over to him, slipping her arms around his neck. The warmth of her body and the silk of her skin were far too evocative.

"Every night with you is good," she said softly.

He caught her arms, kissed her lips swiftly, and then stepped back. "Thank you. And I feel the same. But if we don't leave now…"

"Gotcha!" she said. "Clothing. Great stuff. Let's get some."

They both dressed quickly, and Kylie packed an overnight bag with a speed that almost surpassed his—and he was accustomed to traveling at a moment's notice.

In minutes, they were in the car.

Jon glanced over at Kylie. "Are you okay? Going back there? Especially since…"

"What did Ben tell you?" she asked.

"Two tourists went missing. They found one in a giant jack-o'-lantern."

"And you think the other is in Brenda's wall?"

He looked ahead at the road and shrugged. Then he said, "Yes."

"What is it about Halloween?" she murmured.

"Hey, we're still on Thursday night. Halloween is Sunday."

She turned to him as he drove and said, "Halloween in Salem is pretty much all of October. And it can be so wonderful—music, performances…"

"And a town filled to the brim with tourists. People who love the holiday. And this year…people who like to find their prey. But I'm asking you, are you okay going back? You're amazing, and you have learned to shoot and have taken self-defense classes, but—"

"But I'm still a civilian, and I'm not trained."

"Trained or not, your ability is an amazing asset, Kylie. A killer could have gotten away if it weren't for you."

She smiled at him. "Jon, I want to stop bad things from happening whenever I can."

"But you were almost killed," he reminded her.

"I had you. I *have* you," she said softly.

Jon hoped it was enough.

"So, what's the plan?" Kylie asked.

"We're going to get a room at the Hawthorne. I don't have the office on Essex Street anymore, but I love the hotel. It will be about five a.m. when we get there. We'll check in, I'll get you to the police station to be with Brenda, and I'll join Ben at the house and see what they've found." He shrugged. "This is a local matter, you know. Ben is a friend, and he won't have a problem with me assisting in his investigation. But as of now, this isn't a federal case. And while most cops are great to work with, every now and then, you hit one who doesn't like federal interference."

"Or that of weird people who see things through the eyes of others," Kylie murmured.

"Ben must be the lead detective on this case—the missing tourists. We'll be fine. But—"

Kylie swung in her seat to watch him as they drove. "Of course, we could find out that someone *did* get into Brenda's historic dream home and set her up to find a ridiculous Halloween prank. And, Jon, you're the agent. And you're good—incredibly good at what you do. I won't put myself in any danger," she promised.

He smiled and nodded and then said, "After I meet with Ben, and we calm Brenda down, I'd like to try and find Obadiah Jones. I have a feeling he might be looking for me."

Obadiah Jones was an old friend.

A very old friend.

A dead one.

When Jon had been just a kid, Obadiah had been the first spirit to approach him—and with no-nonsense determination. Obviously, not many people would listen to a dead man.

But a child had been kidnapped.

Thanks to Obadiah insisting that Jon act—even if he was only a kid at the time—the crime had been nipped in the bud.

Also thanks to Obadiah, Jon had learned in his later years that he wanted to serve his country so he could then go into law enforcement.

"I'd like to see Obadiah, too," Kylie said.

"We'll search for him together," Jon promised and managed a smile. "We'll search for him or he'll find us, I'm sure."

"Yep."

"I wonder if he can help."

"He's an amazing spirit," Kylie said. "If we need help and we're not just looking at a Halloween prank, that is."

They had traveled no more than forty-five minutes before Jon's phone rang. He answered it through the car system.

"Jon Dickson."

"Jon," Ben said.

"And Kylie. I'm here, too, Ben. And thank you," Kylie said.

"No," Ben said wearily, "Thank *you*." He hesitated. "We definitely found our second victim. And, sadly, this wasn't any kind of a Halloween prank."

Chapter 3

At the hotel, the young desk clerk looked at Jon and Kylie as if they were a bit insane. Of course, it was five in the morning, and they'd both forgotten just how *crazy* Salem could be at this time of year.

"There's nothing left? Nothing at all?" Jon asked, even though he knew the answer. *Haunted Happenings* drew people from all over the world, not just the country. He should have thought about it, and he should have asked Jackson to have Angela Hawkins Crow—Jackson's wife and executive second—to work on securing a room for them.

"I'm so sorry," the young woman told them. "We're in the middle of *Haunted Happenings*. We don't have any rooms."

Kylie smiled. "Right. Of course. You have likely been sold out forever. But a friend of mine was going to try to check in tonight—"

"What's the woman's name?" the young clerk asked.

"Brenda Riley," Jon answered.

"Oh, yes. She's at the police station—not in a bad way. I mean, she didn't do anything wrong. I'm sorry. I actually know Brenda. We went to high school together. She was definitely upset tonight. Arlo, from the evening shift, told me that she'd been holed up in a booth in the back of the bar for a few hours. I didn't come on until just after she left. Arlo said that a nice officer came for her, and Brenda went with him. She wanted a room, but even if I'd been on, and even for Brenda…there's nothing I can do. One of the managers gave away the last of our hold-back rooms yesterday. Now I'm worried about Brenda, too. Um, maybe you should try calling her?"

"She's okay. She just had a frightening experience," Kylie said. "And the officer who collected her is a friend. I will give her a call now. I didn't do it along the way because I hoped she'd somehow managed to get some sleep. Anyway, thank you so much for your help."

The girl at the desk shuddered and then spoke softly as if someone might have come into the lobby or the walls had suddenly grown ears.

"I don't know what happened with Brenda, and I don't know all of what happened in town, but even amid Halloween craziness, the police have been showing a marked presence on our newscasts and the streets. There was a murder. And you know we always have tourists. So many people are really interested in and saddened by everything that's happened here. But at Halloween…well, I'm guessing maybe we have a demented tourist on the loose. Anyway, please be careful while you're here. Not that bad things haven't happened before, but—"

"We know," Kylie murmured.

"Halloween might just bring out the worst of the worst."

Kylie thanked the woman and stepped away from the desk. Jon followed her through the quiet lobby.

"I should have called Brenda back," Kylie said. "I'd hoped maybe she was sleeping, and that Ben had come by and made sure she was tucked safely in a room and getting some rest if he didn't take her to the police station as you suggested. Of course, she grew up here and has dozens of friends in the area. I'm sure she can stay with one of them. Since you grew up here, too, I'm hoping you know where we can try to get a room."

"Devin still has the cottage, but it's a bit out of the way." He was referring to Devin Lyle, now wife of Craig Rockwell, better known as *Rocky* to the Krewe. Devin wasn't an agent, she actually wrote children's books, but she had worked with the Krewe during the case that had brought Jon and Kylie together.

"Too far away for being in the heart of the investigation here. We should stay at Brenda's house. *At* Brim House," Jon said, watching Kylie carefully.

Her eyebrows flew up.

"With the bodies?" Kylie asked him.

"Kylie, once I get there, they'll already be taking the bodies away. Ben wants me to see what they found, but they've already had to break away more of the false wall. You heard him when he called. Forensics will work the house for several hours, but the electricity came on after midnight, so…"

"Jon, we don't know—"

"Are you afraid of ghosts?" he asked her dryly, a crooked smile in place.

"Ha-ha. Okay. So, what do we do now?" Kylie asked.

She appeared to be awake and fresh, even alert. He wasn't sure how. She'd slept in the car for a while, and then she'd driven to give Jon some time to nap. But they'd still only had a couple of hours of sleep each.

It had actually been an easy trip. They'd shared the road with a few truckers and not much other traffic, and manipulated highways that were often bumper-to-bumper with comparative ease.

"I'll drop you at the station. There's a breakfast place not far from it. You can spend some time with Brenda while I work the crime scene with Ben. See what she can tell you."

"You think she knows someone who might have done something so horrible? I think the clerk must be right. Whoever abducted and killed those two tourists must be…well, I think, someone from out of town."

Jon was quiet for a minute, prompting Kylie to speak again.

"Jon, there's no way a friend of hers did this."

"I think whoever did it is from Salem. How else would they know not only the legends but also the layout of a house, the architecture, the times of day people wouldn't be around, and when it might be possible to carry a corpse in unseen?" he asked her.

She shook her head and reached for her phone to call Brenda.

Jon waited patiently as the women spoke. Brenda's voice came through clearly because of her agitation and nervousness.

"You're here!" Brenda said.

"Yes, we came to the hotel—" Kylie replied.

"Booked. Booked solid."

"Yeah, we found that out. Jon is going to bring me to you—"

"I'm at the police station."

"Right. We know. You and I can get some breakfast. Jon said there's a place near the station—"

"The Witch's Whistle," Brenda said.

"Right. We'll get something to eat and let the police finish at the house."

"Finish? How can they finish? I was supposed to have workers out today. A crew was supposed to come in to clean, and then I was going to see if anything needed to be shored up. They did an inspection before the sale. But, then again, I didn't think there would be false walls in the house. Still, I guess if you're going to stick a dead man in your walls, you wouldn't pull a permit to do it." She laughed nervously, and Jon heard it.

"But the police asked me to stop people from coming in today. They're hoping to clear the house by tomorrow."

"Okay, let's get something to eat and figure out what to do next," Kylie said. "Jon is going to drop me to be with you, and then he'll head on over to Brim House."

"His friend, that detective? He's very nice," Brenda said.

Kylie glanced at Jon, and they both smiled. "Yes, he is."

"Unless you commit a crime," Jon said softly. "Anyway, let's—"

"Right. We're heading out, Brenda. I'll see you soon."

Kylie ended the call, they waved to the night clerk, and then turned to walk to the car.

The woman stopped them. "You reached Brenda?" she called out.

"I did." Kylie turned. "She's fine. Thanks again for your help."

Jon paused outside the hotel, waiting for Kylie to catch up. The sun was just coming up. He'd parked by Salem Common, and he thought about the city and its beauty. Fall brought an outstanding assortment of colors to the Earth. The oldest building in the area dated back to 1664— the Pickman House—and others still stood from the latter 1600s. Salem offered parks and museums and higher education, along with a rich maritime history.

And, of course, witches.

History and shops abounded that relayed information or sold souvenirs dealing with the tragic history of the people who had been incarcerated and executed. Now, many Wiccans lived in the city. Some were offended and others were not by the many signs, logos, and so on that featured witches on broomsticks. None of it had ever bothered Jon. He'd been happy to play John Proctor in his high school production of a play written by his teacher—one that stuck solidly to all known records. He loved the museums, too. And as a kid, he'd attended all kinds of classes offered by the Peabody Essex Museum.

He really loved Salem. And he understood. It was the past, but it was also the present. And because of the past, the present was vital and vibrant—one couldn't separate the two.

Kylie watched him, and he gave her a sheepish grin.

"Sorry. We should get going."

"The bandshell on the Common is decorated," she noted.

They could see the Common from where they stood, and the bandshell and various areas of the green where Halloween events were ongoing or being set up was indeed festive. Unfortunately, every organizer of every event would be nervously checking their decorations now, hoping no bodies filled their pumpkins.

"I know you love Salem," Kylie said softly.

He smiled at her. "So do you. You came here again and again."

"But it's not my home as it was yours."

"Kylie, we both know that bad things can happen anywhere. Let's worry about Brenda for now. By the way, you didn't answer me. I don't think it would hurt if we just stayed at Brim House. What do you think?"

"Okay. Though, I don't know how soft the beds are." She laughed.

"We'll find out, won't we?" He winked.

She nodded. "I guess we will. What about Brenda?"

"She might be better off staying with a friend."

They got into the car and drove out to the station. He noted that— murdered tourists or not—the streets were already starting to show life. It was barely six a.m. None of the museums would be open yet. Not even what he knew to be Kylie's favorite: The Salem Witch Museum, where she thought they managed to convey the history—and the horror—without sensationalism. The craze might have been brought on by greed, different people coveting their neighbors' land and letting that be known to children. Or by simple hatred, jealousy, or even blind fear and ignorance. The woods had been filled with dangers back then, and people believed that the devil could dance in the darkness and lure away the unwary.

Someone once theorized that hallucinogens in the wheat may have caused the frenzy—but that had never seemed true to him. Nor had it ever been proven. Why would so few have been affected?

And, of course, thousands were hanged or burned to death worldwide during the period, each accused of witchcraft.

"Hey, everything okay? I think I may be doing better than you," Kylie said softly, placing a gentle hand on his arm as he drove.

He smiled at her. "I'm fine. Are you okay?"

"Not in anyone else's skin at the moment," she assured him.

"Or thumb or big toe?" he teased.

"Nope. I'm not seeing anything." She hesitated. "I've learned now to see the dead, to take control while talking to them...I'm really not afraid of ghosts. Those I've met want to do nothing but help. But this thing...seeing through others' eyes, I have no control at all."

"Maybe one day. Then again, maybe not. Perhaps it's just supposed to be," Jon said lightly. "And I'm sorry. It must be so frightening."

"It's okay when I wake up beside you."

"Then you're just always going to have to wake beside me."

"That works."

He smiled as he drove to Margin Street, where the station was located. He intended to park and go in, but Kylie stopped him. "Jon, it's a police station. I'll be fine. Drop me in front and get to Brim House."

"Okay. I know Ben got them to hold the bodies until I got there—or the skeleton and the body, whatever it may prove to be."

"Go do what you need to do. Don't worry about me."

Jon kissed her goodbye and watched as Kylie got out of the car. Waving to her one last time, he headed to the scene.

Police officers stood around the perimeter of Brim House when Jon arrived, but Ben Miller—maybe with a bit of intuitive talent of his own—walked out to the front porch just as Jon parked down the street.

As he walked up, he spoke to several uniformed officers standing on the porch, watching for interference.

Crime-scene tape marked off the entire yard, and several cars were already near the house.

Neighbors had come out to watch the procedures, as well. He noted that people watched from the houses to the left and the right—and also from all the way down the street.

Of course.

"I guess they're all asking what's going on, huh?" Jon said. "Have they been out here all night?"

"Most of them emerged in the last few hours. The older gentleman to the right—a Mr. Charles Flannery—demanded to know what was going on."

"And what did you tell him?"

"That it was an ongoing investigation and I wasn't at liberty to say anything right now. But he insisted that I tell him if Brenda Riley was all right. He seemed very concerned."

"I guess she must have met them all when she came out to see the place," Jon murmured. He looked down the street, making a mental note to run the plates of every person who watched, and look into every neighbor who lived there.

"I assume you're right," Ben told Jon. "Come on in. The medical examiner is ready to take the corpses—or the corpse and the bones and fragments, anyway. We called in a forensic anthropologist. She came up from Boston and is waiting at the morgue." He grinned. "Apparently, she doesn't mind playing with bones. But she didn't want to come out to the house to deal with the newly dead."

"There *is* a difference," Jon said lightly. "A very old set of bones likely means no one to be devastated when they find out someone they loved is dead."

"And no smell," Ben said. He drew in a breath. "The fresh corpse hasn't been there for long. So, unless you're close… In another day, if that wall hadn't caved in, Brenda Riley would have likely been down in the basement looking for the critter that crawled in and died." He waved toward Brim House. "Come on in and see for yourself."

Jon entered the house. It was a mix of styles. He thought it had been an old saltbox originally, with the basic square of the entry and parlor sitting over the original foundations. He'd need to study the architectural plans, but he thought the den might have been added on in the mid-seventeen-hundreds. The stairs in the parlor area had clearly been part of the original house, leading to the second floor. Across from the den, a modern kitchen had been added at some point, along with a dining area.

Jon followed Ben through the main house to the den. He could quickly see the portion of the wall that had given way. Old wallpaper—perhaps from the 1800s—had covered it. But at the area where it had broken through, he could see that new wallpaper had been added at some point.

When the false wall first went up, Jon thought. Whoever had discovered the passage had removed one of the boards to add a new corpse and then simply replaced the board that had been removed and smoothed the wallpaper back over it all.

The wallcovering was deteriorating. He saw slits and holes in many places, making it easy for the killer to replace the board and paper and not have it stick out like a sore thumb.

Jon could easily see how Brenda simply leaning against another board would have meant her crashing through. Especially since the integrity of the boards had already been disturbed.

She had seen the skull first.

Lights blazed in the house now from the ceiling fixtures and two electric sconces on either side of the entry door. The police had also brought in two bright lights they'd aimed at the narrow space stretching the length of the room behind the false wall.

The skull sat at a level that made it appear as if it were attached to the bones underneath. It had become wedged against a brick in the structural wall, and the old fragments of what looked to be a dress kept some of the bones together. But Jon could see many had fallen and lay on the floor, as well.

Behind the skeleton lay a dead woman, her head hanging. The body was standing only because the same wedges in the brick that held the skull also kept her propped up.

She had brown hair and, in life, he reckoned, had been about five feet six inches tall and weighed perhaps a hundred and twenty pounds.

He slipped on a pair of gloves and glanced at Ben.

Ben nodded toward the other side of the room.

"Dr. Samantha Ridgeway," he said. "She's done what she can with the corpse in the wall. She didn't mind waiting for your arrival."

The doctor was a tall, slim woman with chestnut hair wrapped up in a bun. She had a narrow face with good features that resulted in an attractive and professional appearance.

Jon walked over to the medical examiner, ready to shake her hand, remembering that his hand was gloved.

So was hers.

They shook anyway.

"Jon Dickson," he said.

"These guys just call me Sammy," she told him.

"May I lift her head?" Jon asked.

"Yes. And then we'll start removal. My assistants are waiting in the kitchen. Ben has seen to it that there are dozens of crime-scene photos, but he wanted to wait until you got here to do anything more. By that time, we were all assembled with the house roped off anyway, and we knew it wouldn't be long."

"Thank you. I deeply appreciate the professional courtesy," Jon told her sincerely.

He wasn't sure how it would help that he had seen the old bones and the fresh corpse as they had been discovered, but it had been a damned decent courtesy.

He very gently reached past the skull to lift the head of the woman behind it.

The body was ice-cold. There hadn't been electricity in quite some time, and it was the end of October in Salem. The temperatures had been dropping. He detected the smell of death now being so close to her, but the cold had also kept decomposition from progressing as quickly as it might have otherwise. She'd been about forty, he thought. Nothing marred her body, and he found no obvious signs of death—no bullet holes or knife wounds.

"The other woman, the one in the jack-o'-lantern, was killed with poison," Sammy said from across the room. "I believe this will be the same."

"What poison?" Jon asked.

"Strychnine. The victim's stomach contents held a mixture of fruit juices—and her blood alcohol level was high. We believe the killer invited her out for a drink."

Jon nodded and looked at Ben.

"Do we have that warning out?" he asked.

"Just thirty minutes ago. We strongly cautioned our visitors—and locals—about accepting drinks or food from strangers." He let out a breath. "Finished up a video for the various news agencies about twenty minutes before you got here. Oh, that's when the rest of the neighbors appeared on their porches and started watching from the sidewalk, too."

Jon took a step back. "Thank you," he said again. "Have you questioned the neighbors? Did they see anyone coming or going?"

"So far, we got nothing. The only people they saw were the realtor and Brenda Riley. Brenda came in at night, saw what was behind the false wall, and tore out of the place. We have a call into the realtor now. Her name is Mandy Nichols. She's worked here in town for almost twenty years and has a sterling reputation."

"I've heard the name," Jon murmured. "May I speak with the neighbors?"

"Be my guest. See if you can get anything," Ben said. "We're not giving out the names of the deceased. We *are* saying we've found the bodies of the missing women. And, as I said, we warned people about the poison. Aside from that, we're not disclosing anything else."

"Do we *know* anything else?" Jon asked dryly.

"Well, we know this victim was found in a wall in a home that was just purchased. And when I asked Brenda about it, she told me that she posted on social media about buying the place, so anyone could have known. She also wrote that her first day in the house would be today."

"I believe," Sammy said, speaking up quietly, "that the body was put in the wall not long before your friend, Brenda, arrived. Strychnine isn't as fast-acting as cyanide or some other poisons, so the killer kept the victim somewhere until…well, until she died."

"Thank you," Jon said again. "Someone had to have seen something. I'm going to find out who."

"We'll start removal and see what we can uncover. And it's interesting. I'm wondering who these other remains belong to, as well. I believe the skeleton has been here a long, long time, but…"

"I saw a serious nick on one of the rib bones—one that showed through the fabric. The dress was cotton—organic—so most of it is gone, but…I believe our forensic anthropologist will agree with me that whoever she was, she was stabbed—which is likely our cause of death. I don't know if that can help in any way with what is happening here today, but…"

"Everyone deserves justice," Jon said. "No matter how long it takes."

"Amen!" one of Sammy's assistants—a big man of about thirty—said. He winced. "Sorry. I guess, well…what you said—justice, no matter how long it takes—it resonated."

Jon nodded and started out of the house, passing two officers standing guard on the front porch, sternly watching for any trespassers.

He looked to the right and saw an older couple—a tall, thin man of perhaps seventy, and his wife, a tiny woman roughly the same age.

Not enough strength to manage the task, he thought.

He waved to them and then looked to the left. An attractive young woman in her early thirties, dressed in jeans and a rock band T-shirt watched, along with a young, tall, lean man with long, dark hair. He could have been in a rock band. He was slim and wiry but appeared young and strong.

Jon walked toward them.

"She's in there, right? The second tourist? We just watched the news conference," the man said.

"I'm afraid so. Or at least we believe it's her. We'll need to wait for an official identification."

"We told the police we saw Brenda walk in all happy last night," the woman told him. "And then she ran out—white as a sheet—a few minutes after. She seems so nice. What a horrible thing to have happened to her."

Pretty damned horrible to the victim, too, Jon thought.

But he understood. Brenda was about to be their neighbor.

"You didn't see anything yesterday morning or afternoon? Anyone arriving with a bundle, or…anyone arriving at all, for that matter?" Jon asked.

The young woman frowned. "Oh!" she said. "We have a door camera. It might have picked something up. I can bring up the video on my phone. I forgot—I totally forgot. I mean, it's for *our* door and our front yard, but it might have caught something."

"Please," Jon said. "Anything would be greatly appreciated."

She started fumbling with her cell, her fingers slipping as if she were too nervous to hold it properly.

But he waited.

"Ginger, do you want me to help?" the young man asked.

"I've got it. I've got it," Ginger said, walking down the steps from her porch to hand Jon the phone.

"You just push the little arrow," she said. "Oh, and the time button is on the top—you can put it on fast forward."

"Thanks."

He owned and used the same phone, so going through the motions wasn't difficult. But even using fast forward, it took some time to get through the day.

But then he stopped the video. And went back. He looked harder, wincing inwardly.

He glanced at Ginger. "I'm going to need to take your phone for a bit. I promise we will return it to you. The detective in charge needs to see this."

"You're not the detective in charge?" she asked, frowning.

"No, come on. Look at the suit," the young man said. "He's FBI."

Jon nodded. "Yes, I'm FBI. I'll—"

"But I need my phone. It's my life," Ginger protested.

"I thought *I* was your life," the young man said, shaking his head with dry humor. "Ginger, let him take the phone. He's FBI."

"Thank you. We'll see that no harm comes to it," Jon promised.

He turned and headed back to Brim House. Once inside, he saw that the bones and bits and pieces of old fabric, leather, and buttons were being assembled on a tarp. Sammy was in the hole with the murdered woman's corpse.

Ben stood by, watching, but quickly turned to Jon when he approached.

"You got something?" he asked, looking surprised and anxious.

"I do."

Jon showed Ben the video.

Ben stared at him, disbelieving.

"A clown?" he exclaimed, the words all but exploding from him. "How in the hell do we ever find a damned clown at Halloween?"

Chapter 4

"I'm calm," Brenda told Kylie. "I've—I've calmed down. The police have been great."

They were still just down the block from the police station at the little breakfast place that, like so many others, played on history for its name: Witch's Whistle. Police officers on break occupied three tables in the charming restaurant.

It had been a good choice.

"Of all the things that might happen," Brenda continued, "I didn't think some horrible monster breaking into my house to leave a corpse would be one of them. We even had structural engineers in—the place is sound. Yes, a house was there during the trials, but only the foundation and the four walls of that house remain, so…oh! Maybe curses are real."

"I don't believe curses from hundreds of years ago can cause havoc today. But people *can*," Kylie said. "Brenda, the police will be done in the next few hours. Jon wants us to stay in the house."

Tears suddenly welled in Brenda's eyes.

"Kylie, I've dreamed of owning such a place all my life. The minute we met, you and I talked about the history of the town. And not just the witch trials—the giant elephant in the town—but also the seafaring and the skirmishes here before the actual start of the American Revolution. And so much more. To own something that lives and breathes history…"

"You still own it. And it's still amazingly historic," Kylie said. "That doesn't change just because a horrible human being did something heinous."

"No, it adds to the *ghost* history," Brenda said and then winced. "*Is* it cursed? Am *I* cursed for buying the place?"

"Brenda, let's give this some time, okay? The police are already on the trail of whoever killed the poor tourist in the jack-o'-lantern. Jon is here now, and he's determined. Between them, they will solve this. The house didn't do it—a horrible person did."

Brenda nodded and then absently tried to drink from her empty coffee cup. Kylie saw their waitress and smiled, motioning to her and asking her to come over.

The young woman cheerfully returned Kylie's smile and quickly refilled Brenda's cup.

"Brenda, we are curious—not about a curse—but about any people who might want to play upon a curse. I quickly refreshed myself and brushed up on a little of my history online earlier. The original owner of the house that stood on the lot was a man named Josiah Brim. His wife, Elizabeth, was accused of witchcraft and arrested. Governor Phips officially ended the trials in May of 1693, and Elizabeth—like the others who had been held—was released. After her family paid her bills for being incarcerated, of course. But by that time, she was so sick, she died the following week."

"In the house," Brenda said, nodding. "Josiah said he cursed the town and the very earth and all those who caused the insanity that resulted in the death of his wife. He was so angry that he ordered the house razed to the ground and then he moved to Boston. But when they were tearing the house down, they left four walls—the main section of the house—as I mentioned."

"Though not the den with the false wall," Kylie mused. "That wall went in when the house was rebuilt."

"Right." Brenda let out another sigh. "That was when Ezekiel Johnson murdered his wife, Mary. They found her dead in the yard with one of her kitchen knives in her back. Ezekiel proclaimed his innocence until he was executed—also cursing the very ground and everyone in Salem."

"Well, he might have been innocent. And he might have been guilty," Kylie said. "Jon will be happy to tell you that very few people admit to being guilty—unless it's to a lesser crime so they can strike a deal on a more major one."

"Why did I buy this house and think everything would be okay?" Brenda moaned. "Once we get to the 1800s, Priscilla Alcott supposedly murdered her husband, Michael. I never found records on that, but some of the ghost tour guides like to feed the rumor that Priscilla murdered her husband to avenge Mary Johnson, who might have been a great-aunt or great-great-great-aunt or cousin or something. I don't know. The murders were fifty years apart, so *no one* knows for sure. And Michael's body was never found, so it was just speculation. Of course, the neighbors shunned her."

"Well, in the early days, in many convoluted ways, many of the colonists were related in one way or another. Especially by the 1700s," Kylie said. "Maybe…"

"Maybe?"

"Perhaps that's Michael you discovered last night."

"Ah, seeking justice and popping in on me."

"Oh, wait. I'm sorry. It can't be Michael. The body belongs to a woman. Brenda—"

"Let's move on up," Brenda said bitterly. "To the 1900s. That was when Fisher Smith was suspected of being a serial killer before we really even recognized multiple murderers. It was right about the same time that H. H. Holmes was terrorizing World Exhibition attendees in Chicago in his murder basement."

"Nothing was ever proven with Mr. Smith. He was a crotchety, sixty-year-old man at the time and not well-liked. He made a good scapegoat for rumor mongers," Kylie reminded her.

"Eric Mulberry, a tour director, disappeared in 2001," Brenda said softly. "The last stop on his final tour was Brim House. Kylie, maybe it *is* cursed. Maybe the very ground is afflicted."

Kylie shook her head firmly. "Eric Mulberry finished his tour. People saw him and spoke to him at the bar afterwards. He was angry about something to do with his rent. He probably just moved on to another city. Adults are allowed to disappear if they choose to do so. The tour guide could be alive and well and living in New Mexico—or even in another state or country. And you're forgetting—strong men and women, *leaders*, those who fought against the British taxes for badly hurting families, also lived in the house. And in both the Revolutionary and Civil Wars, soldiers needing long-term care and rehabilitation were looked after by the McMahon family, who owned the house sometime in the eighteenth or nineteenth century."

"That's what I thought was so wonderful," Brenda said. "All the good that was done there. And just think, they were caring for all those soldiers with a skeleton in the wall."

Kylie glanced at her watch. She'd been with Brenda for almost two hours. Thankfully, no one working in the restaurant seemed to mind that they had hoarded the table for way longer than it took to order and consume a meal.

Still, she was anxious. It was time to move on.

But to where?

"I think, with your permission, that Jon and I will stay at the house tonight. But—"

"You're worried about me. That's okay. Don't be."

"It's your house. We can pick up a blow-up bed. Jon and I can sleep anywhere on anything. Really. I understand the man who owned the property before you set up the kitchen and one bedroom—"

"Right."

"You can stay at the house in the room. We can—"

"No. I'm not staying there. I can stay with a friend from work for the next few nights. At least until I can get something on my own."

Kylie was silent. She thought about telling Brenda that she didn't have to give up her dream home, but then again, it might be unnerving to live in the house. Not because it was allegedly cursed or haunted, but because a recent murder victim had been stuffed into her wall.

"Who are you staying with?" she asked.

Brenda smiled. "Abigail Ventura. She lives in an apartment building with a doorman and lots of security. And I know you and Jon. You'll have the police patrolling the area, and Jon will be investigating Abigail's background and will have someone checking on us." She hesitated and frowned. "You think it was just the house being used, right? You don't think it was done because someone is after me?"

"I doubt it. Two tourists disappeared and were then found dead. It's someone with a sick sense of Halloween and an even sicker sense of being human," Kylie said. "The house was merely convenient."

"I hope you're right," Brenda murmured. Her expression changed, and she looked past Kylie to someone who had just come into the café.

Kylie turned. A woman walked toward them. She was attired handsomely in a blue suit with a flounced blouse and wore trendy high heels. Her hair was a soft brown and swept engagingly around her face, falling just to her shoulders. She was dressed for business—her appearance different from the many costumes Kylie had seen already— and attractive. Kylie thought she might be in her mid to late thirties.

"Mandy!" Brenda said.

"Oh, Brenda."

The woman rushed forward, and Brenda stood. The two embraced, and then the woman pulled back and looked at Kylie.

"Forgive me. I'm Mandy Nichols." She held out a hand for a shake.

"Kylie Dickson."

"I was the realtor who sold Brenda Brim House," Mandy said. "The media picked up on the police chatter, and I was going to call you. Oh, Brenda, I'm so sorry. We had inspectors in there and everything. No one saw that false wall. I can only imagine what you've gone through...I am so sorry! Of course, I'll do everything I can to take the house off your hands. I feel so terrible. I can even see if I can get some financing to buy it myself."

"Oh, my God, it was horrible," Brenda said. "There was a body behind the skeleton, and they think it was the missing tourist. She was murdered, too."

"It's what we suspect, anyway," Kylie murmured.

"Again, I'm so sorry. There were cop cars all over the area. Naturally, the media got involved, and a spokesman or a cop or someone gave a statement. I am appalled. You just took possession of the house yesterday. I will take it off your hands—"

"Mandy, that's not necessary," Brenda said.

"Are you in law enforcement?" Mandy asked of Kylie.

"No, no. I'm a docent at a museum, actually," Kylie said. "I just love Salem. Brenda and I, being old friends...well, you know how Brenda loves history."

She wasn't sure why she didn't mention that Jon was a federal agent. They wouldn't be lying to anyone, but it just didn't feel right.

"Well, thank you for being such a friend," Mandy said.

"Did you want to join us?" Brenda asked.

"Oh, no. But thank you. I just came to pick up a to-go order. It may be *Haunted Happenings*, and close to Halloween, but a fellow on Charter Street insisted that we have an open house today. He thinks tourists will fall in love with Salem and want to buy his place." She sighed softly. "Not if tourists keep disappearing, though. Especially," she added, wincing, "being discovered in Salem houses. Anyway, I'm on the clock. I just saw you here and...Brenda, I really am so, so sorry."

"Mandy, you arranged for a great price and did some amazing negotiations on a property I loved," Brenda said. "Please. You mustn't be sorry in any way."

"Well, I guess we'll talk at another time," Mandy said. "Kylie, so great to meet you. Thank you for being here for Brenda."

"That's what friends are for," Kylie said. "And nice to meet you, too."

Mandy waved to them and then headed to the counter, taking possession of a large bag and paying the clerk.

"She's amazing."

"I've heard she's been a realtor for a long time," Kylie said. "In fact, I'm pretty sure I saw her picture on billboard ads before."

Brenda nodded. "She was a teenager when she started. Well, not the legal parts and whatever, but her parents were realtors. She took over their firm when they retired and moved to Nevada."

"I guess she knows her stuff," Kylie murmured.

Her phone vibrated, and Kylie saw that Jon was calling her.

"Excuse me," she murmured to Brenda.

"Jon?" Brenda asked.

Kylie nodded.

"Hey," she said softly into the phone. "Anything?"

"Preliminary," Jon told her. "The bones have been there forever. The remains and the body of who we believe is the missing tourist are on their way to the morgue. A forensic anthropologist is coming in from the college to study the bones, and they'll do carbon dating."

"Um," Kylie said, glancing at Brenda, "anything more?"

"Oh, yeah. A clown brought a giant bundle—presumably the woman's body—into the house."

"What?"

"Yep. You heard me. Brenda's neighbors—a woman named Ginger and her live-in boyfriend, Kenny—have a camera alarm. It's for the front of their house, but it catches a corner of Brenda's yard. You can just see a clown—big, frizzy wig. Giant red nose. White outfit with red circles. And huge, red clown shoes—carrying something toward the house."

"Great," Kylie murmured.

"The forensic team is just finishing up now. They're hoping to find something. The only people who should have been in the house in the last months are the realtor—Mandy Nichols—and the few people she showed it to. The previous owner, a fellow named Kenneth O'Hara, hasn't been inside since he bought it five years ago. He intended to create a bed and breakfast, but his wife got sick, and he spent the next few years at her side. And then the pandemic hit. He lost the desire for what he intended to do and just wanted to sell the place. So, he handed it over to the realtor. When Brenda bought it, he ordered that the kitchen be updated, and a new bed be put in the largest bedroom upstairs. Brenda wanted what remained of the old—antique—furniture, and O'Hara simply wanted out. The crew that put in the kitchen was only three men, and two local workers delivered the bed. So we can trace the fingerprints in the house to those people for elimination, though it may take some time. Anyway, I'd like to see if we can find our old friend. But I'm not sure about leaving Brenda alone."

"Right. I just met Mandy Nichols, by the way. She popped into the café to pick up a to-go order. She's working an open house today. She told us the police gave a statement to the press?"

"They did. What was she like? Never mind, we'll talk when you're not with Brenda."

"Right."

"Okay, so…we need to make sure Brenda's safe, and then I'd like you with me."

"Of course," she agreed. They couldn't bring Brenda with them to find Obadiah Jones.

"So?"

"Hmm?" Kylie murmured.

She was surprised when Brenda—who had been watching her as she listened—laughed and spoke to exactly what Jon had been saying.

"He wants you to be with him when he's doing whatever he's going to do, but he's worried about me," Brenda said. "Seriously, I'm calm now. In fact, I'm angrier than I am scared. So, here's my plan. I have a key to Abigail's apartment, and the guard at the desk knows I'm allowed to be there. You can see me all the way there if you'd like. Make sure I'm locked in, and then you can head on out. Abigail plans to take off work early, so I really won't be alone for that long."

Kylie laughed softly. "Brenda, it's still morning. You will be alone for a few hours, at least."

"And I may sleep."

"Okay. But you have my number. And Jon's. And—"

"I know how to dial 911." She smiled. "Which, of course, I could have done last night, but I really didn't know what I had seen. And…"

"It's okay," Kylie assured her. "You did the right thing. You got out."

Brenda nodded, and Kylie remembered that Jon was still on the line.

"Pick us up," she told him. "We're taking Brenda to a friend's to get some sleep."

"On my way."

Kylie paid the tab, and they headed out to the street to wait for Jon to come by. Brenda thanked him effusively once he arrived, and Jon assured her that it was fine. At Abigail's apartment building, he left the car near the curb and insisted on seeing the guard at the front, then walking up to the apartment with Kylie and Brenda. Before they entered, he went through the apartment room by room.

"Should I be scared?" Brenda asked him.

"Nope," he told her. "Can't help it. I'm an agent."

"Well, good. And thank you. Again, I—"

"Get some sleep. We'll talk later," he told her.

Brenda smiled, nodded, and walked with them to the door, letting them hear her as she turned the bolt into place once it had closed again. After heading back to the car, Jon drove them back towards town.

Kylie looked at him. "*Should* she be scared?" she asked.

"I really don't think so," he said. "But it never hurts to take precautions."

"Right," she agreed. "We're going to the cemetery, I take it?"

"We *are* going to the cemetery. I think Obadiah knows we'd look for him there."

"He doesn't hang out there often."

"No, but he knows we'll be looking for him. Trust me, Obadiah knows what happened here. And he is passionate about stopping people from being hurt."

"All right," Kylie murmured. She looked out the window as they drove. "A clown," she murmured.

"A clown at Halloween. Who would notice?"

"You talked to all the neighbors?"

"No one saw anything. We just have video from Ginger Radisson's phone. The police have it now. They'll enhance it and study it as much as they can, but if you're going to run around committing a crime, there's really nothing like a clown suit to use as a disguise."

"And there's no time like Halloween to wear it," Kylie murmured. "Anyway, Brenda was pretty depressed. She thinks the house and the grounds are cursed. She went back over all the suspected crimes. In one instance, supposedly proven since there was an execution in the case of Ezekiel Johnson, she determined the house was afflicted."

"I was born in Salem," Jon reminded Kylie. "Someone always owned the Brim House when I was a kid, but nobody ever lived there long. For years, a company that wanted to create a historic attraction owned it—another wax museum or something. They never got the funding for it, so the place stayed vacant. Then the man who sold it to Brenda bought it. He wanted to create a bed and breakfast at the house, but his wife got sick, and he lost all heart for the project."

"I know all the stories. The ghost tour guides always pointed out Brim House as a haunted location. So, naturally—"

"You being you, you did all kinds of research."

"I did. But that didn't really help. Heck, it's hard to prove recent cases. And going back hundreds of years, it's almost impossible. Brenda just told me some of them, too, though."

Jon nodded. "But then there is this," Jon said. "We are in Salem, Massachusetts. And again, even back when I was a kid, museum researchers did all kinds of investigations on the house's history. Salem has changed through the years, and people change. It is far more commercial today than even when I was a kid, but people need to work and make money. And I don't think people should ever forget the trials. Some want to embrace the past. Others want to wash it away. And in my mind, it's always best to admit and see the bad."

He smiled and continued. "Some think it's fine that we have commercialism as well as history. That it includes all our souvenirs, the witchcraft stores, the museums, and more. Growing up, I knew several practicing Wiccans. But they aren't the dance-with-the-devil witches that were suspected of witchcraft in the 1600s. As it stands today, Brim House wasn't there during the witchcraft trials in 1692."

"Right, but the foundation existed for another place they razed. The builders used the foundation and a few walls to construct the new building, so I guess the basement was the basement during the trials. The house that stands there now was built by a man named Josiah Brim. Which, of course, is why it's called Brim House. He had a family, and to the best of everyone's knowledge, they lived there happily enough until they left the area. As I told Brenda, good people lived there, too. Not just the reportedly bad ones. But, Jon, at this point, there's nothing, right? No suspect in the picture at all? It could have been anyone from anywhere, dressed up in a clown outfit."

"No," Jon said quietly.

"No? You *do* have something?" she asked, confused.

He took a breath, shook his head, and then glanced her way. "Nobody visiting the area did this, Kylie. Whoever it was probably heard the stories about the house all their life and researched it just as meticulously as anyone might. I'm going to assume it was a man—the size of the clown and the strength needed to manipulate a body behind a false wall *and* behind other skeletal remains lends better to a male. They had to know about the house. And everyone in the neighborhood. He knew when people were at work or occupied. And when he could slip into the home without being seen. He didn't plan on Ginger Radisson's front door camera, but he did plan for the costume just in case someone saw him. Someone local did this."

"But what local?" Kylie asked.

He hesitated again. "Someone who grew up near the house with access to it would be my guess. Maybe even someone who, as a kid, snuck in all the time. And somewhere along the line, learned about the false wall."

"Not a friend," Kylie said quietly. "No friend would—"

"I didn't say a friend. But we both know killers often wear costumes—not clown costumes, per se, but disguises that make them look like ordinary people."

"So, what's your plan?" Kylie asked.

"The neighbors," he said flatly. "If I keep talking to all of them, someone may come up with something. Anyway, I'm going to park here. We can walk."

"The place will be spilling over with tourists," Kylie warned.

"Yes, but we're together." He winked. "We don't even need to pretend that we're talking on our cell phones."

The cemetery was beautiful. The markers weren't big or elaborate, but those of the long dead had been re-etched, and a plaque that described the opening of the cemetery and where to find important graves had been hung. Nature had taken over in places, and tree roots had broken through some stones.

As Kylie had thought, the place was crawling with tourists. Tour guides were out and about. Candy was being given out at several of the businesses near the cemetery. And children with bags that had ghosts, witches, or pumpkins on them—with a superhero here and there—collected their sweet treasures.

Kylie stopped, looking down sadly where a small child had been buried, and thought that some things never changed. Parents loved their children. Such a loss must have been devastating, no matter what century such a thing occurred.

She felt Obadiah before she saw him.

And knew he had set his hand on her shoulder.

"I've been waiting for you two," Obadiah said.

She tried not to turn or be too obvious.

"Do you know something? Can you help?"

Obadiah was the first soul Jon had encountered as a child. A spirit who had been determined to talk to and through Jon, and halt something horrible from happening. Jon walked over and stood next to Kylie, looking down somberly at the grave, as well.

"Hey," he said quietly.

"Hey," Obadiah answered. Kylie smiled. Obadiah did not speak at all as one might expect a Puritan man to talk. He'd told her once that he'd been hanging around as a spirit much longer than he'd hung around in life and that it was easy enough to bring his use of the English language up to contemporary times.

"We need help," Jon said simply.

"I know. I must start out by telling you that I only learned of the missing women through the television at a pub where I occasionally like to hang out. And while it never occurred to me to watch Brim House, I did see what happened with the woman stuffed into the giant jack-o'-lantern meant to designate stage left for the theater group."

"Who was it?" Jon asked hopefully.

Obadiah was silent for a minute and then he said, "A werewolf."

"A what?" Jon and Kylie said together.

"A man dressed up as a werewolf, anyway," Obadiah said patiently. "I tried to follow him, but he ran through the shops. And while I would think that everyone would notice a werewolf, people have been dressing up here all month. I lost sight of him in the Pedestrian Mall on Essex Street. And since then, I've been hoping to find the truth behind the costume. But…I knew you would come."

"You knew? But until Brenda called…" Jon began.

"Brenda?" Obadiah said. "Ah, the young woman who purchased Brim House?"

"Yes. She loves history. It was a dream come true for her to own the place," Kylie explained.

"I saw the news today. They found a second victim and think it's the missing tourist."

"And some very, very old bones," Jon said.

"Old bones? Interesting," Obadiah said. "I'll speak with some friends. I was dead by 1693...along with Elizabeth Brim and many others. Sarah Osbourne, Ann Foster... Even more died in prison because their debts couldn't be paid. Elizabeth made it home, but her death is still directly due to the craze that swept through here—along with others, seldom mentioned. History and those who study it agree that twenty were executed—but I doubt anyone living today knows the true death toll because of the jails and the lack of sanitation, disease, and malnutrition."

"Obadiah, we know what you suffered—"

"I'm not asking for pity. I was just explaining that I don't know who the bones belong to. But I do have friends on this side of the field, more or less," he said, grimacing ruefully. "I will do my best to see what I can discover."

"What I would really appreciate is you making a few stops," Jon said.

"A few stops?"

Jon smiled. "Places I can't legally enter."

"Ah. You have a suspect for me to spy on?" Obadiah asked.

"Several. I could be very wrong, but I think it's someone who knows not only the house but also the history of it and more. They know what's going on. When someone is there. When the sale took place. When to slip in and leave the corpse," Jon said.

"The killer was dressed up as a clown this time," Kylie said.

"So we're looking for a clown and a werewolf. Could be one and the same," Obadiah murmured. "Unless, of course, there is more than one killer."

"I think the costumes put us in a very difficult position," Jon said.

"Yes, indeed. Halloween—and a killer who loves dressing up. Hard to find among the hundreds who will be in costume for parties tonight, tomorrow night—and definitely on Halloween itself," Obadiah said. "I will do what I can and speak with some friends. But is Brim House where you'd like me to start?" Obadiah asked. "I doubt they'll put another corpse in the same place."

"As of now—or at least that we know about—no one else is missing. Detective Ben Miller with the local police is working on some information regarding the victims. He feels they may have been targeted and were followed here to be killed in the confusion of *Haunted Happenings*. I don't agree. I think they were victims killed while on vacation. Naïve and accepting of the wrong new friend. Or *friends*," Jon told him. "And spying on the neighbors, well...that can't hurt."

"As you wish. But, remember, the first victim was found at the edge of a makeshift theater," Obadiah reminded him.

"Something anyone might have seen as a good site to leave a body, and one to draw sensationalism," Jon said. "But Brim House is different."

"Different it is." Obadiah smiled grimly. "I accept the mission. I will spy on those who share the street with Brim House."

"And," Kylie said thoughtfully, "maybe see if you can come up with anything that connects any of the people in the area today with those who owned the house in years past."

Both Jon and Obadiah looked at her curiously. She shrugged. "People get things in their minds. Maybe they're trying to take revenge for something that happened in the past."

"Why would someone seeking revenge kill tourists?" Obadiah asked.

Kylie looked at Jon. "Maybe they live someplace else now but had ancestors who lived here?" she said, her words more of a question than a statement.

"Maybe," Jon said quietly. "We'll call the office. Ben is looking into the victimology, but Angela is darned good at finding details. Okay, so…"

"I don't go into bedrooms," Obadiah said.

Kylie smiled. For a minute, she could see him as a Puritan. He was dressed in the customary black breeches and jacket associated with the period, and his expression was stern.

"Good to know in case we're fooling around at Brim House," Jon said.

"Oh! More than you needed to tell me, sir," Obadiah said.

"Hey! We're married now," Kylie said.

"Ah. Well, congratulations!" Obadiah said with pleasure. He lifted a hand in farewell and was off to follow his mission as he saw it. He paused and turned back.

"Still, I do not spy in bedrooms."

He left them then. As Kylie watched him go, she thought that if others saw him, they'd think him dressed for Halloween and nothing more.

But others did not see him. They moved about the cemetery with guidebooks, seeking the famous—and the infamous.

She heard Jon on the phone and turned to look at him. He'd said that he would call Angela, and he'd wasted no time in doing so. But as he listened, he looked at Kylie with his face knit into something of a frown, his eyes intense.

She waited for him to finish.

"Jon?"

He let out a breath, shaking his head. "You should be an agent," he told her.

"What? Why?"

"Angela was already checking on the victims—the police department got a positive ID. Ann Chester and Lily Franklin, both here from Indianapolis. They weren't just friends—they were cousins. And their great-grandparents moved to Indianapolis at the beginning of the 1900s. Their great-grandmother—who moved the family to Indiana—was a descendant of Ezekiel Johnson."

Kylie arched a brow in surprise. "But wouldn't that make her a descendant of Mary Johnson, as well?"

"No. I guess the ghost stories—or even the court records—don't include the fact that he was married before. His first wife passed away from a fever. So, Kylie, you might not be so far off with your revenge theory. But that puts tons of people in Salem in danger. These things happened so many years ago. Dozens of people might be descendants of those suspected of—or who really *did* commit—the murders. We have a lot of family trees to trace."

"But if whoever did this is somehow seeking revenge for things that happened hundreds of years ago—"

"That person is probably descended from someone he sees as having been wronged and left without receiving justice. The very concept is crazy. But it is a direction for us to go."

"Right, got it," Kylie said. "We're looking for a werewolf who might also be a clown, who might be descended from a victim of Brim House."

He looked at her gravely. "I need you to start on research."

"Oh?"

"I have places to go, people to see," he told her.

"Really?" she said.

"No, I don't really have places to go, but I *do* have people to see. You'll get to see them, too, though. Because I have them coming to Brim House."

"People are willing to come to Brim House? Even with the latest press conference?"

"Yes. Which makes it all the more interesting to see those I want to see at Brim House. Possibly, right in the den."

Chapter 5

Archives were exhausting, but Jon knew Kylie loved research. He found it intriguing, but it was also tedious—sometimes telling and often not.

They had stopped for lunch before heading for the house, knowing what to expect.

The place was, beyond a doubt, a mess.

The false wall was gone, and the old brick of the structural wall was sturdy but shedding crumbling bits and pieces of dust about the den.

The forensics team had trampled the floors when they finished up, seeking whatever clues they might be able to find to identify whoever had entered the room carrying a dead woman.

But the kitchen was clean and in good repair. When Jon and Kylie checked upstairs, they discovered a brand-new bed in one room, along with linens and towels still in their store wrappings. Someone had swept the floors up here, but the bathroom attached to the bedroom—probably added in the 1970s—wasn't up to date with modern standards. It was usable, in working order, and clean, however.

"Okay?" he asked Kylie.

"Sure," Kylie said, giving him a shrug. "Brenda told me negotiations on the work needing to be done had been fierce—though not because of her. She had simply wanted the house in the worst way. You don't know Brenda that well, but she's passionate about history and justice—and, honestly, all good things. When she bought the house, she knew the *bad* things about it, of course. But she was more enchanted by all the good things. It was here during the Revolutionary War. Before and after, the owner at the time had been fierce in siding with—and helping, we believe—the people's written protests regarding the tax punishments the

British intended after the Boston Tea Party."

Jon chimed in. "Salem was part of the Massachusetts Bay Colony, and the world was witch-crazy at the time. The first person hanged for witchcraft in the Colonies was Alse Young—in Windsor, Connecticut. No, it didn't turn into hundreds being accused, but the point is bad things have happened everywhere."

"I know that. And Brenda knows that. But buying the house, well, it meant a lot to her. She is a proud New Englander. She considers the history of Salem, Massachusetts to be so rich—tragic, but rich—because she especially loves the fact that the country's founding fathers knew the history here. It influenced them, and they made sure that such things as spectral evidence would not be allowed in the courts. And that all citizens had absolute freedom of religion."

"I should have asked before. What does Brenda do for a living? Teacher...researcher?"

Kylie shook her head. "Brenda is artistic. She works for a major retailer as a window designer. But she has wanted to write a book about the events here and how they influenced the Age of Enlightenment for ages. The thing is, she didn't much care about the state of the house. Mandy Nichols fought to make sure that when Brenda bought the place, she'd be able to live in it right away. That any repairs, updates, and whatever else could be done at her leisure. So, yeah, workers were due to start today. But, of course..."

"What about Internet?" he asked.

Kylie smiled. "Oh, there's Internet. Brenda worried about that before she even thought about electricity, trust me. Now that we have both, I can set up my computer in the kitchen. Or the bedroom if you'd like me out of the way."

"You don't need to be out of the way—another person listening to everything is good." He glanced at his watch and smiled at her. "The Flannerys are due in about twenty minutes."

"The next-door neighbors? They agreed to talk to you? But you said no one saw anything, and since they know the missing woman was found *dead* here, you'd think that..."

"They'd refuse to talk to an agent who is not even officially on the case?" he asked.

Kylie grimaced, dug her computer out of her bag, and headed into the kitchen. But she had barely left the parlor before she returned, looking toward the den.

"What?" Jon asked.

"I thought I…well, I thought Brenda saw something in the wall on one of the wooden support beams or columns, whatever they are."

"Something more than a skeleton and a body?"

"The wood. It's old, I know, with all kinds of scratches from construction, and it's splintering in areas, but…is it all right if I go into the den and look?"

"Of course. The forensic team finished with the place. We wouldn't be in here if they hadn't. I have my penlight, though most of the false wall has been torn away."

Kylie nodded and walked into the den.

"Brenda entered the house filled with excitement," Kylie said. "And she had a big flashlight. She came through the parlor and walked into the den, then just leaned back to see what was in the room. Right there," she said, indicating a place where bits of the false wall remained. "When she leaned on it, it broke, and she looked to her right and saw the skull first. It seemed to be staring at her from its empty eye sockets—or so she thought. Then she realized there was something behind it, and the light caught on the victim's face. She saw flesh. But right above that…there. Jon. Put the penlight there, please?"

He did as she asked. At first, he saw old wood. Scratched from the time the building had been built over its old foundations, ragged from chisels and tools, chipped and splintering. There were scratches on it, but moving closer, he thought Kylie might be right. There were deeper scratches in one little area right above the point where the head of the murdered woman had lain. They formed strange crescents, like half-moons, one next to the other.

"What do you think that means?" Kylie asked.

"I don't know," Jon said, pulling out his phone to snap some pictures of the etched marks. "But I do believe you're right. The marks are recent, certainly. Most likely put there by the same person who, apparently, knew about the wall and the skeleton and thought he'd add to it. I'm sending the images to your email. Download them and see what you can find."

"And you're sending them to Angela, too, right?"

"If they mean anything, one of you or a brilliant young person in our tech department will discover *what*."

There was a knock at the door.

Jon went to answer it, and Kylie followed behind him.

"Mr. and Mrs. Flannery?" she asked.

"I think so."

"I still don't believe they wanted to come over here."

"I don't think they know I'm unofficially on the case. And I don't think they'd care one way or the other. It seems they want to see the house. Curious, huh?"

"You think one of them dressed up as a clown and carried a woman in?"

"No. They're older and not in great health. But they may have seen someone hanging around the house at a different time—or may even know who was related to whom in this area."

He opened the door, and as expected, Mr. and Mrs. Flannery stood on the stoop. They were a handsome older couple. Both slim. And Jon had noted earlier that Mr. Flannery—possessor of a fine head full of snow-white hair—wore a medical alert bracelet. He didn't believe that anyone who might need help quickly could have dressed up as the clown he'd seen on Ginger Radisson's phone video. The clown had appeared bigger, too, a bit taller and broader across the shoulders. Of course, the clown costume had been billowy, but that wouldn't explain the shoulders. And Mrs. Flannery was a little bit of a woman. She might have been someone's accomplice, but she surely hadn't been the clown.

"Please, come in. And thank you so much," Jon said.

The couple entered.

"Mr. and Mrs. Flannery, I'd like you to meet my wife, Kylie," he said politely.

"Charles Flannery, my dear. And my wife, Emma," Mr. Flannery said.

"My pleasure, and I'd like to thank you, too," Kylie said.

"I don't know if we can be of any help," Emma Flannery added. "We *are* out in the yard often enough. It won't be long before the flowers are all gone, and we both love our garden. But we didn't see anyone coming or going from the house. Ah, well. Anyway, we didn't have far to come."

"That's true," Kylie said, smiling.

"Are you a police officer, too, Kylie?" Emma asked.

"No, just a museum docent," Kylie assured her. "But the owner of the house is a friend of mine."

"Brenda. Such a lovely girl," Emma said sadly. "Of course, we met her when she was looking at the house. We were so pleased. She didn't intend to rip it up or create a silly sensationalist business or anything of the sort—she just wanted it because she loved it. And now…"

"Now, it will be a vacant sore thumb again," Charles said sadly.

"Brenda may yet keep the house. We'll have to see," Kylie said.

"Well, anyway, we don't need to stand in the doorway. Let's sit, shall we?" Jon suggested. "The sofa is very old, but the room has been swept, and there are a few chairs we can drag over from the mantel area."

"As you wish," Charles said.

"I'm working in the kitchen," Kylie called. "If anyone needs me, I'm just through the doorway there."

She disappeared. Charles and Emma sat on the sofa. Jon thought it was a nineteenth-century piece, but he wasn't an expert. He brought one of the cushioned chairs that faced the mantel over and sat, looking at the couple. They looked back at him expectantly.

"I assume that, having lived next to this place for years and years, you know the history," Jon said.

"Of course," Charles said. "Our house belonged to my parents and their parents before them. I grew up next to this *haunted* house. My grandmother used to tell me tales about Fisher Smith, the man they suspected of being what we now call a serial killer, but no one was ever able to prove it. You'd hear about a murder in Peabody or Revere or elsewhere, and it always happened to be somewhere Smith had gone for the week or a weekend on business. Maybe there is justice we don't know about sometimes. He was killed rather ridiculously by a falling icicle. Of course, people were still murdered. But not close to here, and not on days when he happened to be exactly where the murders were taking place. Nowadays, you people would have nailed him."

"One can only hope. So, your families have been here forever?"

"Oh, no, not forever," Emma put in. "My father passed away when I was a little girl, still living in Boston. My mother brought me here when I was about five because the game company offered her a good job."

"And my family came up right after the Civil War. Like Emma's family, my grandfather was offered a job, and there wasn't much left in Mississippi at the time," Charles said.

Jon wondered if that meant they were lucky. They might not be on a killer's radar. Though, so far, it seemed the killer was targeting women.

Easier to offer a woman a poisoned drink.

"I am so sorry we can't help you more," Emma said sincerely.

"I'm curious. Charles, you said you've lived here all your life. Is much of the block the same? People leaving their homes to their children?"

"Ah. These days, kids can't get going fast enough for a down payment," Charles said, shaking his head sadly. "But I do believe that many people, with homes like these, try to keep them in the family. Now, the house to the other side…that's a bit newer. It wasn't built until around 1890. There's still some family history there, but somehow, that lovely Ginger girl bought it from a fellow who had been there for about twenty years. And before that…I think the place changed hands a lot."

"Ginger didn't *somehow* do anything, dear. She has a great job. She works in computer graphics," Emma told Jon. "Very talented. I understand she helps create some of those phone games young people are constantly playing these days."

"There is a lot of money in that, or so I hear," Charles said.

"The house is hers? Not hers *and* her boyfriend's?" Jon asked. "His name is Kenny Innes, I believe."

"That is correct. Well, I think one day they will both own it," Emma said, smiling. "He is a nice young man."

"He always offers to help shovel the driveway when we're bombarded with snow," Charles said. "Very helpful. Has a job. And a respectful fellow, too. Ginger could do much worse."

"What about the other neighbors?" Jon asked.

"Let's see," Emma murmured. "Down the block on Ginger's side you have Ned Olsen. Poor sad fellow—a widower. They were childless, and when his wife passed…I think he's just waiting to go, too. His grandfather bought the house after World War II. His family hails from Annapolis, I believe. He was a military man. And across the street, you have the Matheson family. Joe and Darleen and their little ones, Pearl and Amber, ages six and seven. Delightful. Now, Darleen's family *does* go way back, but as far as this place goes…I don't know. And the next home…"

Charles wrinkled his face in thought.

"It's the Daily place," Emma said, taking her husband's hand affectionately.

"Right! Robert Daily and his wife, Gertrude—or Gertie, as they call her. They have owned it for about thirty years. They came up from Boston, too. But those two…well, they had a litter."

"Charles, that's not at all nice," Emma chastised affectionately. "Six children. Two sons are in the military, and all three daughters moved back to Boston. They spend half their time there, and they're lucky to be able to do so. They have one son, Calvin, that still lives in Salem. He has an apartment by the wharf, I believe. But when they're gone, he comes home to take care of Woof-Woof."

"The dog," Charles explained as if the name weren't self-explanatory.

"And that's it on the block. We are lucky. Close to town, within walking distance. But these lots are large, and the three houses face each other. And please, believe me, these are the nicest neighbors anyone could want."

"That is great to hear. And thank you so much," Jon said.

"Are you talking to everyone on the block?" Emma asked.

"I hope to," Jon said.

Emma shook her head sadly. "If anyone knows anything, they would have come forward. These are good people."

"I'm sure. But, sometimes, we forget what we know. And when someone asks, things can come to mind. But I do thank you, so sincerely." He stood, and the couple did the same.

"We're here if you need us in any way for anything again," Charles said. He patted his pocket. Jon had given him a card earlier, and the gesture indicated that he still had it on him. "I have your number here. If we think of anything, we'll call."

"Thank you."

Charles looked toward the den. "That was where—?"

"Yes," Jon said.

"Sad thing, sad thing." Charles shook his head. "You know, we love *Haunted Happenings*, adore the music, the art, and the fun. It shouldn't be marred like this."

"No," Jon agreed.

"Charles, quit looking. We're not going in there," Emma said. She took his hand and headed toward the door. "Good day, Mr. Dickson."

"He's Special Agent Dickson, Emma," Charles corrected her.

"And you're welcome to call me Jon," Jon said, amused. But he was relieved when they walked out the door.

Next up was the young man watching Woof-Woof.

He arrived minus the pooch about three minutes after Charles and Emma Flannery left.

"I admit, I agreed to come because I've never been in this place," Calvin Daily told Jon, seated on the sofa where the Flannery couple had been earlier. He was quite tall and lean, and appeared wiry, fit, and agile, with a thatch of light brown hair over his eyes, and an easy smile. "When I was a kid, we raced by this place at night. The ghost tours still come by, of course. And we've heard all the stories. Funny—they were often about the dead buried in the walls, screaming for help. Well, not funny. Ironic. Anyway. To a kid, the place was terrifying."

"Calvin, you walk Woof-Woof. So—"

"Sorry. That's a ridiculous name. My mom gave it to the dog. I did not."

"Hey, we all name our pets what we like, right?" Jon asked. "The thing is, you walk the dog. So, that means you're out on the street."

"I had to work yesterday. I didn't get here until after dark. The only person I saw at the house was the new owner, and she was looking at it the way I did when I was a kid. Like I wouldn't want the place on a silver platter."

"But what about in the last days or even weeks? Did you see anyone here?"

"Yeah, last Saturday. They delivered a bed. And the realtor lady was out here with two workers, and…yeah. There was a cleaning crew, too. A lady and a man, on…mmm, Monday. Saw them come and go, and then saw the realtor lady check the lock on the door before she left. None of them was here without her, though."

"Any cars that shouldn't have been on the street here more than once?" Jon asked.

"None that I saw," Calvin told him. He shook his head. "You know, people on this block have a love-hate relationship with the place. Ghost tours trample by—but they are careful. They never let anyone step foot on anyone's property. It's famous. Hey, when I order a pizza, it comes right away. Everyone knows the address. I am sorry. I just don't think I know anything that can help you."

"I appreciate you coming over," Jon said. "Sometimes, what people don't see is as important as what they do. By the way, what do you do?"

Calvin Daily made a strumming motion. "Musician. And *Haunted Happenings* is a happening time for me. Lots of gigs. That's why…well, I wasn't on the street all that much. Just made sure Woof-Woof got fed and ran around a bit. I'm also a part-time game designer. But playing gigs is what I love to do."

"Well, thank you again. Hope to see you play someday."

"Cool. You like music?"

"Of course."

"Best rock guitarists?"

"In my mind? Hendrix, of course. Gilmour, Page, and Clapton."

"All right, man. So, sure, cool, hope you make it to something. I'll be on Essex Street, Halloween night. Playing with the Wolf Howlers. I didn't pick that name, either."

As Calvin was leaving, Kylie emerged from the kitchen. They talked briefly, with Kylie telling Calvin that she'd love to see him play someday and they'd try to make it Halloween night. Then Calvin looked at Jon as if he were a lucky man.

He was.

When the door closed on Calvin, Jon asked Kylie, "You found something?"

"Maybe. And maybe not."

"Well?"

"I don't think the half-moons are a symbol of any kind."

"No?"

"I think they form a letter. I think they're the letter *M*."

Chapter 6

"M—as in Mary," Kylie explained to Jon. "What Angela discovered was that the women who went missing and were later found dead—Ann Chester in the jack-o'-lantern, and Lily Franklin in the wall—were descendants of Ezekiel Johnson from his first wife. If someone is trying to right an old wrong, they might have etched out the letter M. The killer was saying the murder had been done for her—for Mary."

"Okay, that makes sense. But Ezekiel Johnson went to the gallows after being convicted of her murder. Mary is in holy ground. And as far as I know, her spirit did not remain. And I believe we would know—Obadiah would have said something."

"Do you think the first wife—?"

"She couldn't have had anything to do with Mary's death. She was already dead. A widower could remarry, but don't forget, this was Puritan New England."

"But she had children. We know that much. Angela traced the ancestry. And Mary had children, though from what I've seen on the ancestry sites, they spread out like wildfire—west and out of the country."

"This is confusing," Jon said. "Unless…"

"What?"

"Maybe the children of the first wife didn't believe that she died of natural causes. Perhaps Ezekiel didn't kill Mary. Maybe one of his children did. *That* could be why a descendant of Mary and Ezekiel wants to kill the descendants of the first wife? As crazy as that may be. But killing and placing bodies in jack-o'-lanterns and walls indicates a warped mental capacity to begin with."

A knock sounded at the door.

"See what you can find out about Ezekiel's first wife's death. Find out if he knew Mary before his first wife died," Jon said, walking to the door.

"Uh, sure. Just like that. Pity they aren't walking around. We could just ask them," Kylie said.

He arched a brow and headed to the door. "You're right. Obadiah would know if Mary or the first wife—"

"Her name was Teresa."

"He would know if one of them had remained, and he would have said so. But he might know more about what happened. He would have been long gone himself, but…"

"We need to see him again."

"I think he'll see us. He's spying on the neighbors, remember?"

"Right. Get the door. I'll get back to research."

Kylie quickly returned to the kitchen. She was listening as he talked to the neighbors. And she was curious. She didn't want to be drawn from her computer out to the interviews, but she did like seeing the people before they left.

She keyed in her first search—her effort to discover the timing of Ezekiel's first wife's death.

She half-listened as Jon spoke with the widower, Ned Olsen. He sounded like a tired and very sad man. She peeked out before he left and saw him stooped and weary. She found herself feeling sorry for him. Wishing there were something someone could do for him.

The Matheson family came next—not the little girls, just Mr. and Mrs.—Joe and Darleen. They gave the same report that Calvin had given. A truck came with two men who brought up the new bed. They had also seen the cleaning crew—and noted the realtor dutifully locking the door before leaving.

Kylie didn't go out to see the Mathesons. Her search had turned up the records she needed.

Teresa Johnson had died in 1685.

Mary Abbott had become Mary Johnson in 1686.

Of course, the records didn't show whether the two women had known one another or not, but they *had* both lived in Salem Village.

Kylie stood up quickly, ready to tell Jon what she had discovered. She wobbled slightly as she stood and realized she'd only gotten about two hours of sleep in the last two days. And they had been busy—the afternoon wove into the night.

She stood for a minute and then walked out to the parlor. Jon was just closing the door.

"Well, I don't know if this is our answer or not, but the Widower Johnson married a year after his first wife died," she told him.

"Okay, we may have discovered a motive. Bizarre, but a motive. Now, we have to get back to tracing who might feel that some slight—perceived or real—from hundreds of years ago needs to be avenged."

"Or it might just be a way for a very sick murderer to choose his victims."

"That's possible, too."

"Are more people coming?"

"I spoke with the cleaning crew, the delivery men, and the workers who came to assess what needed to be done earlier today. None were here alone. And according to everyone, Mandy Nichols was religious about locking the door."

"Well, keys can be copied."

"That they can. There is also a back door, but it was bolted, so no one went out that way."

"One thing we know is that a clown brought her in here," Kylie said.

"And Obadiah saw a werewolf put a corpse in a jack-o'-lantern. I was thinking..."

"That we're both about to keel over?"

"Yeah." He smiled. "Let's call it a night. I think we'll be better if we start bright and early. I'm going to give Angela a call. Update her and the tech team doing what they can to trace the family trees—no easy task. They must have thousands of branches by now."

Kylie found herself glancing toward the den.

Jon walked over to her, taking her by the shoulders. "Hey. Are you going to be okay here?"

She smiled at him. "I don't think anything could keep me awake all night."

"Okay. I won't try. I promise."

She laughed and escaped his hold.

"I'll see you up there," she told him.

She thought she would reach the second floor and the room with the brand-new bed, and its clean, semi-modern bathroom, then crash and fall fast asleep.

But she couldn't.

The shower was too tempting.

And that's where Jon found her. The house didn't matter. The world disappeared when he held her close. Because he *became* her world—with soap and steam making their flesh slick. And, as always, the warmth emanating from him. Nothing mattered but the fact that she was in love with him.

Of course, the shower wasn't that big. And when they were together, they laughed, and laughter could easily become passion. When passion culminated, they still lay entwined, and Kylie knew that she would be all right anywhere as long as she felt his arms around her.

She fell asleep quickly.

And it was a deep sleep, one where she didn't dream—if what she did was dream—or where she entered a different world.

Because she did enter that strange stage...

She was looking at the house. At Brim House. Staring up at it, at the windows to the bedroom where she currently slept with Jon. Watching...

Her thoughts were not hers.

FBI. FBI, so tough! Not so tough. Everyone has a weakness.

Close, so close...

Then, the fog swirled, darkness, and...

Kylie woke on a gasp. Jon held her, but even as he did, she heard his telephone ringing. He eased himself from behind her and dug his cell phone out of his jeans.

He answered it quickly and was up in a flash, stepping into his pants.

"On the street? Ran back behind the house? Brim House? Your house?" he asked.

Kylie was up just as quickly. Her overnight bag was on the floor, and she dug into it for a knit maxi dress she could throw on quickly. Jon shook his head at her.

"You are not leaving me alone here," she told him. He'd ended the call and was making another. She realized that he had a direct line to a police officer who had been assigned to keep an eye on the street.

"What is it?"

"I need to move. Fast."

"I can run just as fast."

"Not after this guy."

"He was watching us. From the street. Thinking about you, Jon. Not me. He was thinking that an FBI guy wasn't so tough."

"You saw him?"

"I didn't see *him*. I saw what he saw. Who called?"

"The guy next door. Kenny. He was getting a drink out of his refrigerator, heard a noise, and saw someone running through the space between the yards and into the back. There's a small park out that way, filled with trees, and then you get back to the main street."

Jon was dressed now and tearing down the stairs. Kylie followed him, and he didn't stop her. She quickly realized why. He'd called the officer. And he was already outside, as were the neighbors to the right, Kenny Innes and Ginger Radisson. Kenny wore a robe over his jeans. Ginger looked barely awake and confused as she watched Jon race from the house with the police officer.

"Watch her!" Jon told the guy, catching hold of Kylie's shoulders and pushing her in the officer's direction.

He raced off behind the house.

Ginger and Kenny came down from their porch stairs, Kenny speaking as they did. "Hey, I'm so sorry, maybe it was nothing, but I woke up thirsty. When I was closing the refrigerator...I saw something out of the corner of my eye and went to the window. I think the guy was watching the house, and then he bolted like lightning and took off into back and...well, I said I would tell your husband if I saw or heard anything. Anything at all. I mean, maybe it was nothing. And he's gone now. But I felt I had to call."

"You did the right thing," Kylie and the officer said at the same time. They looked at each other, and despite the circumstances, they each smiled.

"I hope so," Kenny said. "I mean...he's gone. I don't think Jon can catch him, even if he does move like an Olympic athlete."

"Probably not," Kylie said. "Our peeping Tom had too much of a head start. I just hope—"

"That he's not behind a tree, ready to attack?" Kenny asked.

"Jon is too smart for that," the officer replied. He looked at Kylie, and she recognized him. He hadn't been heavily involved in the case Jon had been investigating when he and Kylie met, but they had met at the station. He was a young officer, just starting out.

"Healy," he told her. "Bernie Healy."

"Of course," she said. "Thank you for coming so quickly."

She knew it was right that he was there. She hadn't wanted to be alone. But she didn't know how to find someone on a chase. She wouldn't have been an asset. She would have been a hindrance.

"I didn't make it up; I swear it. And I wasn't seeing things," Kenny told her.

"Oh, Kenny, no. We know you saw something," she assured him. "Are you sure it was a man?" she asked.

"I—um. Well, no. I mean, it was a figure. It's dark out here. I guess I just assumed…"

"You think a woman might be a peeping Tom?" Ginger asked, confused. She had obviously been awakened abruptly.

"Peeping Thomasina?" Officer Healy murmured.

"I just know someone was there."

Kylie wondered. During the regression, when she'd first had her strange experience, she had entered the body of a woman being murdered. She had seen through Brenda's eyes before they came to Salem…

Did sex matter? And was she just incredibly lucky because the dreams told her something she could use to help others? And perhaps, to save her life?

"I'm so sorry. I just…I didn't wake up until Kenny was on the phone," Ginger said. "I don't mean to sound…"

"Half-asleep?" Kylie said. "It's all right. Sorry to disturb you."

"I'm so sorry about…poor Brenda. And you two having to wake up," Kenny said. "But—"

"You did the right thing," Kylie and Officer Healy said together again.

That made Kenny laugh.

Jon came back a few minutes later, winded and empty-handed. "I went all the way to the next street," he said.

"Did you see anyone?" Kenny asked anxiously.

Jon grimaced. "Twenty superheroes, a dozen Disney characters, witches, warlocks, ghosts, werewolves…yeah, people are still partying. It's *Haunted Happenings*. Bars are still open all over town, and there was a midnight tour. Our person could have been any of them. Kenny, thank you. I didn't catch him, but I wonder if he thought you saw him, and that's why he bolted so quickly. Bernie, thank you. If something was going on—"

"Hey, Jon, you know I'll be here as fast as I can. For you guys, anytime. I'll hang out on the street now for a while. We're well covered tonight. You folks can all go back in and try to get some more sleep."

"Thanks again, Bernie. And, Kenny, Ginger. Thank you," Jon said. He set his arm around Kylie's shoulders. They were going back in.

Kylie called out her thanks as well as they walked, wondering if she would be able to sleep again.

Inside, Jon tested the bolt and left Kylie standing by the stairway as he walked around the house, testing every window and the back door.

When he returned, he took her by the shoulders and held her close for a minute.

"Kylie, what exactly did you see?" he asked her.

"The house," she said. "He was looking up at the window, the bedroom window. He knew we were in here, and he knew you were FBI. And he was thinking that even an FBI agent had a weakness somewhere."

"Every man has weaknesses. And any can be vulnerable. Except Superman," he said, trying to lighten the mood. "I saw him on the street tonight. Hey, wait. Even Superman has a weakness. Kryptonite. That's it—every man has his kryptonite. Anyway, we have a lot of work tomorrow. Let's try to sleep."

"Okay," she murmured. She knew—though he would never say it—that he hoped she didn't see through another's eyes again tonight.

They really needed sleep.

One more day.

It would be Halloween soon. And she knew that they both feared what might happen if they didn't catch the killer by then.

They headed up the stairs together, and Kylie stripped off her hastily donned dress and returned to bed. She didn't think she could sleep.

And figured neither would Jon.

He was looking out the window.

"Jon?"

"I'm coming," he said softly. "And it's all right. The killer is calculating how much we know. He apparently knows I'm FBI and that the two of us are staying in Brim House. He's not the kind who openly challenges people. He's plotting his next move. We're safe tonight. And besides my guess—hopefully educated given half a dozen lectures by our behavioral sciences team—on the killer's mental state, Bernie is outside in his patrol car watching, too. And he's a good cop. We can sleep."

He curled up beside her.

And held her.

Miraculously, she slept. And she didn't dream. When she woke, the sun was bright and making its way through the fabric of the drapes.

Jon was already up.

She washed and dressed quickly and then hurried downstairs.

At the entry to the kitchen, she paused.

They already had a visitor.

Not a neighbor.

The ghost of Obadiah Jones sat at the table across from Jon.

He turned to look at her. "Ah, lovely Kylie! Come, sit. Jon has brewed coffee, and it seems I have much to tell."

Chapter 7

Jon indicated to Kylie that she should take a seat while he poured her a cup of coffee. She sat, looking at Obadiah. He remained an impressive figure to her in his Puritan garb—breeches, jacket, white socks, buckle shoes, and sweeping hat. She smiled at him and said softly, "Thank you. You are an amazing friend."

"Ah, Kylie, maybe that's why I've remained all these years. With Jon as a child, and now you and Jon together, you've allowed me to feel as if I have a purpose on this Earth."

"I'm sure you always did," Kylie said.

With more coffee for himself at hand, Jon slid into the seat next to Kylie and nodded to Obadiah.

"First," Obadiah said, "I can verify what you've already learned. Ezekiel Johnson held on for a year—the witchcraft craze was over when he came along, but New Englanders remained prim and proper. Beliefs demanded a year of mourning—at the very least—for a surviving spouse. I spoke with one of my great-nieces, Hannah, who was living at the time. She suspected that Ezekiel had been seeing Mary while Teresa was still alive. And when I suggested that Teresa might have been helped into the grave, Hannah grew thoughtful. At the time, no such thing was suspected—the doctors believed she died from heart failure. Now, of course, an autopsy might have proven otherwise. By the time it was obvious that Mary had been murdered—a knife from her kitchen still in one of the lacerations in her body—Ezekiel's son with Teresa, Hamish, was seventeen. And Ezekiel's daughter, Rebecca, was sixteen. Might one of them have suspected her of their mother's death? Possibly. Would a young person like that commit such a murder in revenge and happily allow their father to be hanged for it? That, I don't know."

"Really digging, I discovered a lot of what we know now online, through various ancestry sites and old Salem records. But I'm surprised the first wife never made it into any of the ghost stories," Kylie said.

"I guess the ghost of a woman viciously killed by her husband, who was then justly hanged, makes for a good story," Jon said. "And, of course, we are talking hundreds of years of history here. So maybe, in time, those telling it have to get to the basics to get it all in."

"Okay," Kylie said. "So, we believe someone is targeting descendants of Ezekiel Johnson's first wife, Teresa. Possibly because Hamish or Rebecca murdered Mary?"

"Possibly." Obadiah shrugged. "None of them remain," he said softly.

"Kylie is great with research," Jon said. "And we also have a tech team back at my headquarters with some brilliant computer nerds. Tell Kylie about the neighbors."

Obadiah shook his head. "I'm afraid I found out little but the usual. Charles and Emma Flannery are like any older couple. They had a bit of a heated argument over him not washing a cup, and she wound up reminding him that he could be a pig and said he should be grateful she was old and exhausted, else she'd be divorcing his ass. But they reconciled quickly and sat on the porch in their rockers, holding hands soon after their discord."

"They don't have the strength, size, or speed to haul in a corpse or to be looking up at our window last night," Jon said. Then, he explained to Kylie, "I told Obadiah about the peeping—disappearing—Tom."

"Oh, I saw all the excitement," Obadiah said. "I had slipped into the Matheson home, but I didn't see the culprit because I didn't know anyone was spying on the house until I saw Jon racing out and the police car arriving. The Matheson couple, again, seem to be like any other. They both dote on their girls. Mrs. Matheson snapped at her husband for allowing the little one to get spaghetti all over everything while she was in the kitchen, but he apologized and told her that they had to let kids get a little messy now and then. Oh, and I saw a family picture of them taken at the Fairy Fae Ball—an event that went on the evening the killer presumably put his victim in the wall. That does not mean they didn't come back and one of them became the clown, but I do think it's unlikely. Let me see... Mr. Ned Olsen. Poor fellow sits in his chair and stares at the television, sipping bourbon all night. Then there is the young man. Now, spying on him was more interesting. He takes the dog out, and he *does* make sure the animal has food and water. But he spends most of his time online with his computer. He even created a Puritans vs. Witches game—not in the best taste, considering the Wiccan population here and the tragedy. But I'm assuming it does quite well."

"Computer games do very well when they become popular," Kylie murmured and smiled. She'd asked Obadiah once why he didn't speak with *thee* and *thy* and other forms of the English language associated with his era. He reminded her that he'd been around for hundreds of years. He was, naturally, up on technology as it came along. He could be capable of mischief, too—messing with the computers of those he followed if he saw them practice cruelty—not something illegal, just cruel.

"Puritans vs. Witches. Calvin is young, tall, and capable of the strength needed," Jon added.

"Can he be followed?" Kylie asked. "Or watched in some way."

"We can do our best," Jon said. "I spoke with Ben this morning. His task force has been following clowns—but we know that our killer changed costumes at least once. I can ask him to get someone on our young Calvin. And if not, I'll see if someone can come up from headquarters. This still isn't an FBI investigation in any official way, but Ben and the guys here don't resent any help. We have a major problem because we're in the middle of *Haunted Happenings*."

"That would be good," Obadiah said. "Now, mind you, the young man did nothing to indicate that he is secretly homicidal." He gave them a weak smile. "I saw him working or playing several games. He's quite good. I think I was born at the wrong time. I would have made a wonderful warrior. A fine member of the Knights Templar."

"The end wasn't too great for Jacques de Molay," Kylie said, grimacing.

"Because Philip IV of France was an avaricious man—deeply indebted to the Templars," Obadiah told them indignantly. He looked at Kylie sheepishly. "Forgive me. I do enjoy reading history books and catching a good documentary when I can pop in on someone watching a fine show."

"It's all right. I agree. The Templars were wrongly persecuted," Kylie assured him.

"Well, I have said what I know. Which helps little, I fear. But I shall keep at it," Obadiah promised. "Oh, and yes, I visited next door. Kenny and Ginger had a bit of a spat over him waking her up when he crawls around the kitchen at night, but…" He paused, wincing.

"But?" Jon asked him.

Obadiah shuddered. "I told you. I don't go into bedrooms. They seemed to make up with a great deal of movement."

Kylie lowered her head, trying not to smile. They all stood, and Obadiah headed for the door. He could, of course, go through it, but he waited for Jon to open it for him and bid them all good luck, pausing to say, "There is today, my friends. Halloween approaches. I don't believe there has been a pointed threat from this murderer, but…it *is* Halloween. And he seems to take great pleasure in dressing up. Halloween, ah. In my day, it was merely the night before All Saints' Day."

"Thank you, Obadiah. We will try hard to stop him before he can kill again," Jon promised.

Obadiah nodded and started down the walk. And then he disappeared into the bright sunlight rising on the late October day.

It would be a good Halloween for New Englanders. Early snows had not come that year. The air was growing colder each day, but the sun made for a nice touch of warmth.

"What's the plan?" Kylie asked Jon.

"I think we should see something of *Haunted Happenings*," Jon said.

Kylie frowned.

"And we're dropping in on the realtor."

"I told you; I met her already with Brenda. She was devastated and said she'd take the house off Brenda's hands."

"At Brenda's loss, I imagine," Jon murmured. "I haven't met her yet. We'll see."

"She was sincerely upset and seemed really worried about Brenda."

"Speaking of, give her a call. Tell her we're sorry since she could be out partying, but she needs to stay locked in tight."

"Will do. She should be fine. People are out in the streets, masked in various ways. Several of the happenings are virtual this year, but businesses are open, so the streets will be filled with musicians and performers and more."

"Exactly. Shall we?" He politely offered her his arm.

"Okay, where are we off to?"

"The Pedestrian Mall on Essex Street." He gave her a wry smile. "We can pay a visit to the Old Burying Point and see if anyone is about, and then stop by the realty office."

"What makes you think Mandy Nichols will be there?"

"She's a saleswoman. She won't miss an opportunity to pick up out-of-towners who find they're in love with the entire atmosphere of the city."

"Shouldn't I be on the computer?"

"Angela and our entire tech team are searching for possible suspects. If I'm right, one of them will be on Essex Street."

"Calvin?"

"He said he'd be playing." Jon hesitated for just a minute. "And, at some time, we'll meet up with Ben and stop in at the morgue."

"Fun," Kylie murmured.

"Don't worry; I'll leave you at the reception area with a police officer while I speak with the medical examiner on duty—and hopefully the forensic anthropologist."

"What makes you think—?"

"An ME is always on. And I'm willing to bet we'll find that the forensic anthropologist is far more interested in bones than in *Haunted Happenings*. I also called Ben this morning and made sure." He winked.

"Oh. Well, okay, then." She stepped forward and took his arm. "*Haunted Happenings*, it is."

As they drove, Kylie called Brenda.

Her friend promised that she was fine and had no intention of going out.

They found a parking spot in the garage. Their subsequent forays would be on foot.

Despite their current situation, Kylie loved the Essex Street Pedestrian Mall. There was so much to seize the imagination. She'd been in the Peabody Essex Museum dozens of times and still found exhibits to explore. One of her and Jon's favorite restaurants—where they had strangely met at a time when she had been overwhelmed by events and had passed out in his arms—was there. Jon had promised they could stop for lunch because they were really at a loss.

She knew he couldn't help thinking that the murderer had to be someone close. Someone who had watched the comings and goings at Brim House.

He didn't know if the killer had intended for Brenda to lean against the wall and expose the dead when she did, but he knew that she would have been in the house by Friday at the latest. And he knew the wall was about to give—he'd just put a body behind it.

As they walked, Kylie remembered why she loved the city so much.

She especially loved the shops. They gave an hour over to the museum, laughed over some of the souvenirs for sale, and enjoyed the imagination that went into so many of the shop windows.

They had lunch at the Cauldron, chatted with Cindy at the bar, and learned that she was afraid—as were several of the locals.

"The police have warned women through the media not to drink with strangers. I still see people in here chatting one another up—and drinking with people they don't know," she told them, shaking her head. "Not me. I go straight home after work."

When she was gone, Jon murmured, "People always think it won't happen to them. That bad things only happen to other people, and that they're too smart to fall for the wrong man."

"Well, hopefully, most of them are now moving in packs," Kylie murmured. Jon glanced at his watch.

"Quick trip to the Old Burying Point," Jon said.

And so, like many of those visiting the city, they headed out to the cemetery, pausing at the memorial that had been erected with granite walls and benches, each seat a monument to an executed victim of the craze. It was both a peaceful place and a somber one. A good reminder to all that mass hysteria and persecution could lead to revealing man's tremendous capacity for cruelty to his fellow man.

They didn't remain long; the day only had so many hours. Then they headed to the office of Nichols Realty.

A young man at the desk greeted them, smiling and cordial. He was, Kylie assumed, on his way to becoming an associate and would have, she was certain, a great sales manner.

He quickly assured them that Mandy Nichols was in and, after a moment, led them to her office.

"Kylie!" Mandy said, rising. She wore another handsome skirted business suit, and Kylie noticed that her nails were perfectly manicured, too. "Oh, no. Brenda is all right, isn't she?"

"Yes. She's fine. This is my husband, Jon. He just had a few questions for you," Kylie assured her.

"Of course. I heard. You're from the FBI?"

"I am an agent, yes," Jon said, nodding and waiting for the women to sit before he took the second chair in front of her desk.

"It's all so upsetting. Brenda is just the nicest human being. And I know how excited and thrilled she was to take possession of the house. I mean, what's going on in the city is distressing enough, but when it comes home like that...I'm still so upset and sorry," Mandy said.

"How many people did you show the house to?" Jon asked.

"I only showed Brim House when I knew the interest was real," Mandy told them. "There was Brenda—and I hoped so badly that she'd get it—and four out-of-town business owners who wanted to do something commercial with it. I have the listing for you. Two of the buyers who came up were from New York, and two were from Los Angeles. They were trying to low-ball on the price. I was delighted when Brenda became the buyer. I have the records if you'd like copies of them."

"Yes, thank you very much. At any time, did you notice anyone taking a special interest when you were at the house?" Jon asked her.

Mandy pursed her lips and shook her head. "At one time, I met everyone on the street. Not that many people, really—three houses facing three houses, the park behind them all...I don't really remember who was where or when. I never let anyone inside the house without being there, and I carefully locked up every time I left."

"We heard you did," Jon assured her. "Are there any other keys in existence?"

Mandy looked perplexed for a minute. "I—I don't know. The last owner had the bolt put in. It's sturdy and strong. I didn't think...well, I didn't think to change it."

"So there *could* be other keys in existence."

"I guess," she said weakly. "Brenda needs to change that bolt immediately." She looked as if she were about to cry. "That is if she chooses to keep the house."

"She very well might," Kylie assured her.

"I really will take it back myself if she doesn't. I'm so sorry. Well, anyway, I'll have my assistant get you the names and addresses of anyone who was in the house—workers, delivery people—"

"I have that list already," Jon assured her. "But I will look at your possible out-of-town buyers."

"Right away."

Mandy left them in her office and returned a minute later with some papers that she handed to Jon. He and Kylie thanked her and stood to leave.

"And now, the morgue," Kylie said. "Are you sure I wouldn't be all right—?"

"The reception area is like any other," Jon said. "But I know Ben and another officer will be there."

Kylie nodded. It was a long drive, but she knew it well. The Essex County Morgue was in Boston.

And as Jon had said, Ben was there, ready to greet them in the reception area, along with a young officer who would remain with Kylie.

"Anything I should know before going in?" Jon asked Ben.

Ben started to reply. But before he could, an attractive woman that Kylie thought to be in her forties came bursting into the reception area from the coolers and autopsy rooms.

"Special Agent Dickson," she said. "I am still surprised that I was able to pull DNA from the bone marrow. Of course, I suppose the way the bones were stashed helped to preserve them. But there's more. I'm stunned that my DNA testing went so quickly. The skeleton and the murdered woman share several markers. Which means that the skeleton, and the new victim, were distantly related."

Chapter 8

Jon hadn't met the woman yet, but he could only assume that she was the forensic anthropologist. And she must have been well-liked and respected here because she evidently had the run of the place.

Detective Ben Miller quickly made introductions.

"Dr. Kathy Morrison, forensic anthropologist," Ben said, "Special Agent Jon Dickson, and his wife, Kylie."

"A pleasure," Dr. Morrison said. "I don't know how anyone got labs working so quickly, but apparently, one of your people set things in motion, and the findings are astounding. Of course, throughout the years, every human being adds new materials. But it's amazing how far we can trace the lines. And while there is no certainty here, the comparison is quite incredible. The skeleton has been in that wall for a very long time. Here we are, hundreds of years later."

"Quite remarkable," Jon agreed.

Behind Dr. Morrison, Dr. Samantha Ridgeway made an appearance. "Jon, come on in. We're ready for you. I don't have anything new to tell you, but you never know. I'm not the kind to mind more experienced eyes on a body. And..." She paused, seeing that Kylie was with him. "Hello, I'm sorry. I don't intend to be indelicate or uncaring. I'm Doctor Samantha Ridgeway, ME, but everyone calls me Sammy. Please, feel free to do so, as well. And if this is something you're working on with Jon, you can suit up and come on in, too," Sammy said to Kylie.

Kylie introduced herself properly, assuring Sammy that she was being straightforward and *not* uncaring.

"And Sammy was right," Dr. Morrison said. "I believe she told you that she suspected a stabbing. The victim, whoever she was, bled to death from several stab wounds. The nicks from a long, sharp blade are visible on several of the rib bones."

"Ben told us you were looking into a theory that, while Salem history is rich with the story that Ezekiel Johnson killed his wife, Mary, your research showed that Ezekiel's first wife left behind teenaged children who might have done the deed and were glad to see their father pay for it."

"It's a theory," Jon said. "Our research showed that the killer's two victims had ancestry that dated back to Ezekiel and his first wife. But we didn't know about the relationship between the two victims in the wall, who were separated by hundreds of years—give or take."

"How could a killer know all this?" Dr. Morrison murmured.

"I don't know. We discovered that Ezekiel probably knew his second wife before his first died—of natural causes. So it was assumed anyway, and so it may have been. It's a long shot to believe that the first wife's teenaged children might have murdered Mary, but what matters is what the killer believes. And a killer—no matter how crazy he may seem—can be extremely bright. I believe this man isn't just a sociopath but a true psychopath. Which doesn't mean he can't function quite normally in nearly all apparent aspects of life."

"Or at least pretend," Sammy murmured. "You're seeing a killer who is bright and organized—and perhaps obsessed with the past."

"Right," Jon murmured. "And on our contemporary victim, Lily Franklin?" he asked Sammy.

Sammy glanced at Kylie.

"I'm afraid my wife is accustomed to shop talk. You can talk freely," Jon said.

"It's all good. I'll be fine with Detective Miller's officer out here if you want to head in. Go ahead. I have my tablet in my bag. I'll be working," Kylie said and glanced at the young man who stood quietly, waiting.

"Oh, right. Kylie, I forgot. This is Officer Todd Linton. He's a good man," Ben assured.

"I'm sure," she said, shaking the officer's hand and then taking a seat as the rest of them followed Sammy and Dr. Morrison into the morgue.

"We can't forget that we're on the trail of a murderer," Jon said quietly. "And I'm afraid time may be of the essence."

"Has there been a threat?" Ben asked.

Jon shook his head. "This man dressed up as a clown and managed to get the corpse into a locked house. The realtor admitted, however, that there *could* be keys out there. Nobody has rekeyed the lock since the last owner bought the house five years ago. Anyway, the killer is running around in costume in the middle of *Haunted Happenings*, so…we need to catch him as soon as possible."

"You think he has other intended victims?" Ben asked.

"Don't you?" Jon replied.

Ben nodded. "Okay, let's do this and get you back out on the street, doing what you do best."

Sammy pulled back the sheet.

Lily Franklin, her Y-incision now sewn, lay on the coldness of a steel gurney.

"Poison causes discoloration but little more. You can see the lividity in her feet—someone stood her up, wedged between the real wall and the false one, soon after death."

Jon nodded, studying the body.

"And as suspected, both Lily and her distant relative, Ann Chester, were given strychnine. Due to her stomach contents, I'm going to say it was delivered through a drink with a great deal of alcohol in it. Strychnine takes a bit longer than cyanide to work, but you don't get the smell, and it is readily available as rat poison. It's a major factor for people with pets because it is so commonly used," Sammy said.

Jon nodded and noticed the scratches on the shoulders, knees, and feet.

He looked at Sammy.

"Post-mortem. From being wedged in with the brick and building materials."

"May I?" he asked Sammy, indicating that he wanted to touch the shoulder to get a better look.

"Of course," she said.

He manipulated the body and could see that, as Sammy had said, the lack of blood rising to the wounds indicated, even to him, that they were post-mortem.

But a curious shape—or *mis*shape to one in particular, drew his attention. He pointed it out to Sammy.

"What caused this?" he asked.

"I can't be certain. The body was really wedged in there."

He glanced at Ben. "I think this mark is a little more defined," he said.

Sammy got a magnifying glass, and they all looked.

"It is possible that the killer etched something there. Again, given the condition with which the body reached the morgue, I can't be certain."

"I think someone was creating an M," he said quietly.

"M—for Mary?" Ben asked. "It's possible. But, Jon, we're still going on a theory here."

"I don't think so," Dr. Morrison said. "DNA is telling. And, yes, we were able to retrieve plenty from the left clavicle. If we needed, the bones—except those nicked by the knives—are intact. Remember, the oldest human DNA retrieved was from a human ancestor who walked the Earth four hundred thousand years ago, taken from a thigh bone discovered in the Pit of Bones in an underground cave in northern Spain. And compared to some of the uses for DNA, comparing the markers of two victims who lived hundreds of years apart seems like a brief span of time. I believe you are right. Someone knows ancestry and thinks they need to carry on their revenge for a historic crime," Dr. Morrison finished.

Sammy looked at her, arching a brow. "Doesn't your family go back to this area for hundreds of years?" she asked politely.

"Well, yes, but I'm not related to Ezekiel Johnson through either wife," she assured them.

"I should see those bones now," Jon said quietly.

The bones, however, gave him nothing. They had been laid out reverently, but if anything had been etched into the woman when she died, it had decomposed along with her flesh and organs.

"She was young," Dr. Morrison said. "Very young. Easy to tell by the development of certain bones."

"And stabbed, like Mary," Jon said.

They talked a little longer, and then Jon thanked Sammy, Dr. Morrison, and Ben for being there. For meeting him, and allowing him into all aspects of the case.

"I'm counting on you to get it solved," Ben told him as the two of them headed toward the reception area. "Tell me about last night. You think the murderer was staring at the house?"

"I do."

"Maybe some random creep, though."

He couldn't explain to Ben that Kylie had seen what happened through the watcher's eyes. Nor could he tell him that their killer was a master of disguise—Obadiah had seen him as a werewolf.

But he could suggest that costumes might easily be discarded, and new costumes worn.

"Gut-feeling, Ben. You know how that works. I know it was him. So, he knows that the police are on to him and that I'm here. I never planned to keep it a secret. Even so, we need to be vigilant tomorrow. I think he might plan to make Halloween his personal religious holiday. And we can't just look for a clown. I believe this guy will change and then perhaps change again, knowing that if he's a chameleon, we'll have a harder time getting a grip on him."

"So damned bizarre," Ben muttered. "That's one hell of a long time to be holding a grudge."

Jon hesitated. "I'm not sure what I think, Ben. All I know is this man is organized and, I believe, very bright. I don't know if he's really so determined to get revenge for a murder, no matter who committed it. But it *is* a way to force him to plot and plan—and pat himself on the back when we fall into his giant puzzle and try to figure it all out."

"But we must figure it out," Ben said.

"Yes," Jon agreed. "We must."

* * * *

Kylie exchanged information with Angela via computer as she waited.

Angela had been hard at work, trying to trace Ezekiel Johnson's children with his first wife. She'd finally found records regarding Hamish Johnson, but none that related to Rebecca. Hamish had left Salem at the age of nineteen, taking up residence in Boston and working as a laborer. He married a woman named Alice Berry, and became the father of twelve children.

Twelve children, their children's children, and so on. And so on. It's like the impossible journey, Angela said in her message.

But I have young, brilliant people in tech with keywords, so I'm hoping to come up with something else. As for Rebecca, the girl seems to have just disappeared from all records. There is a letter in the archives at the museum from a Pearl Cutter to her daughter Agnes that mentions the fact that she believed Rebecca was with her brother in Boston, but I haven't found anything to prove that yet. Then again, we have plenty of descendants of Hamish to try and find, she wrote.

When she died, Mary was a mother to three children: Anne, Samuel, and Brendan, Kylie wrote back.

If this is revenge—say the children believed that Mary killed their mother to marry their father—then the murderers would have been Hamish and Rebecca. If it is revenge, wouldn't it be Mary's children who would want to punish the descendants of her murderers? Which, by our theory, might have been Rebecca or Hamish—or both?

Kylie questioned.

She got back a simple answer.

Yes.

Then Angela quickly typed: *Still, if we knew anything about Teresa's descendants, we'd know who might be in danger. The murdered women were her descendants, and it had to be through Hamish—at least I believe so—because Rebecca disappeared. So...okay, say that Mary Johnson had something to do with Teresa Johnson's death. Someone knew it and killed her. Therefore, I'm thinking that, logically, Mary's descendants are using the past history to kill Teresa's descendants.*

Crazy. Kylie couldn't help but chime in.

Angela added: *Or convenient. Or fun for a sick mind.*

As Kylie sat there, she suddenly wondered about Rebecca's disappearance. She jumped up, causing the officer at her side to startle with alarm, as well.

"I'm sorry. I'm so sorry. I've got to run in for a minute!" she said.

She opened the door to the offices and autopsy rooms. As she did, she thought she was an idiot—she'd never find the right room.

But she plowed into Jon, who was just coming out of a room with Ben Miller.

"The skeleton," she said. "Was the woman young? Around sixteen?"

"I don't know her age, but Dr. Morrison did say that she had been young."

"Jon, I think that the skeleton is Rebecca Johnson. I think she murdered Mary Johnson because Mary helped to cause her mother's death in some way. But then I believe that one of Mary's children came back and killed the person they believed really killed their mother—not Ezekiel, but his daughter with Teresa. Rebecca."

Dr. Morrison walked behind the two men.

"Yes!" she said. "Yes, that would make perfect sense. I believe the timing would be just right."

"Well, there you go," Ben said dryly. "We've solved a murder from a couple of hundred years ago. How the hell does that help us today?"

"Someone is playing on it all," Kylie told him firmly.

"Right," Ben said wearily. "A clown. Fitting, huh?"

Jon walked on past him, taking Kylie's hand. "Thank you all again. And, officer, thanks for keeping watch. I may be paranoid but—"

"Erring on the side of caution never hurts," Ben said. "And we had the overtime in our budget, so all is well."

"Thank you. And thank you again," Kylie said to Officer Linton, grateful that she and Jon were walking out.

"You did it," Jon told her. "I imagine there will be more tests, and I'm not sure how they'll figure it all out, but…you solved the mystery of the skeleton."

"Angela really figured it out," Kylie said.

"Ah. Well, if I were to ask Angela, she'd likely say that you did."

"Once we knew that Rebecca kind of just disappeared into history and that the remains were that of a young woman, it all made sense," Kylie said. "But Ben is right. We aren't any closer to figuring out what happened to our contemporary victims. I mean, there are probably hundreds—maybe thousands—of descendants of both women."

"True."

Jon looked at her.

"But there are only a few descendants of Mary Johnson who might know all about the house. And, of course, it's possible, the story of what happened to Rebecca came down orally through the family via lore. Rebecca's family would feel that she was justified in killing the woman who had possibly killed her mother to marry her father. Mary's children most likely killed Rebecca, possibly with some help from someone older since they would have been young at the time. Teresa's descendants were killed—and the killer is Mary's descendant."

"Still—"

"Someone close," Jon said determinedly. "I believe it's someone we've talked to already. And I can't help but wonder if there's more to the motive than just ancient vengeance. Anyway, it's the night before Halloween. Let's listen to some music."

"What?"

"We're going to check out our friend's gig. Young Calvin Daily, who created the great video game, Puritans vs. Witches." He smiled grimly. "And then we'll go home. We'll have an officer on duty, but he'll lie back in plain clothes in an unmarked car, watching."

"You think the killer might ruin his plan by coming after an FBI agent?"

"If he feels cornered. And I think he just might. In your mind, or *his*, he thought that every man had a weakness, right?"

"Yes."

"Well, my love, I'm afraid that he might be seeing *you* as my weakness. And that's why we'll be extra vigilant and help every step of the way."

Chapter 9

By the time they returned to Essex Street, people had turned out in high numbers—and in costume.

"Maybe we should have dressed up," Kylie said. She liked Halloween—usually. Dress-up and parties were fun.

Generally.

Jon smiled. "As what?"

"Not clowns. Or werewolves. I've already seen a few tonight, but that kid we passed who was about seven years old did it best. I admit, I'm amazed. So many people. And still, many of the happenings were virtual this year," Kylie said.

"Ah, well, we've had record days at airports. I'm willing to bet that our victims—and possible *intended* victims—might not have come to Salem before. But this year, the concept of a city truly embracing Halloween was just too much temptation. There!" he said suddenly.

A band played down the street.

"You can see Calvin Daily?" she asked Jon.

"No, I can see the big banner above the makeshift stage—it says *Wolf Howlers.*"

"Jon, do you think that it could have been Calvin? He seemed nice. And, seriously, little more than a kid."

"He's in his twenties, and people have killed at much younger ages." He stopped, looking at her. "I don't believe that the Flannery couple could have done any of this—neither would have the strength. I believe Charles has a heart condition. That doesn't lend well to hauling around corpses. I think our widower, Ned Olsen, while not a suicidal man, still just wants to join the wife he loved. That leaves Matheson. He's a big enough guy, and God knows enough so-called *family* men have proven themselves to be killers. Then there's Daily and Kenny Innes."

"And maybe none of them," Kylie reminded him.

"They know the house better than anyone."

"But none has a family pedigree that dates back to the early days of Salem."

"We don't really know that for sure, do we?" he asked. "Anyway, let's watch for a bit. The band doesn't sound too bad."

"They sound good. I like them."

They moved closer. The band had gathered quite an audience—because they were good.

They were all in bits of costume. Well, they called themselves the Wolf Howlers, and it *was* Halloween. Calvin was on lead guitar—wearing wolf ears and a furry wolf vest. The keyboard player was dressed similarly, as was the lead vocalist. The bassist had added a tail to his ensemble, and the drummer had an entire wolf costume on—fuzzy pajamas, Kylie thought.

They played old covers and did great with them, adhering to the season with numbers like Blue Oyster Cult's *Don't Fear the Reaper,* Sam the Sham and the Pharaohs' *Little Red Riding Hood,* and Alice Cooper's *Teenage Frankenstein.*

The crowd loved them. And Kylie couldn't help but note that young, attractive women huddled closest to the stage.

Maybe hoping to have a drink with a band member.

At one point, somewhere in the middle of a song from *The Rocky Horror Picture Show,* Calvin saw them in the crowd. He nodded and smiled and looked pleased to find them there. She and Jon lifted their hands in acknowledgement, and Jon gave Calvin a big thumbs-up sign.

"The band isn't bad. How long do we get to listen?"

"They're on for another thirty minutes. I'm going to see what happens after. We'll blend into the crowd, though."

And they did. It wasn't painful at all because the band joked easily between songs and played them all with not just expertise but also the soul that made the difference. At the end, the lead singer announced that Sister Sally Sadist and her Savvy Sisters were coming on next, and then they broke down as the next band came on.

Jon pulled Kylie along with him behind a large advertisement for the various groups.

While there was noise on the street, she could still hear the band members packing up—the drums, it seemed, were being used by all the groups. Guitars and the keyboard were carefully put into their cases.

The crowd had drifted. It would be a few minutes before there was music again.

"Hey, you guys hanging out at any of the pubs?" the lead singer called out.

"Sure!" the keyboardist replied.

"For a bit. Hey, guys, I have a two-year-old at home," the bassist replied.

"I'm heading out. I have real work to afford me being here!" Calvin said.

"Think he's really going home?" Kylie whispered.

"I think we'll see," Jon told her.

Calvin might not have been going home, but he did wave goodbye to his bandmates and weave his way down Essex to the garage.

Kylie and Jon were parked there, too.

"I doubt if we're on the same floor. We'll probably lose him, but..."

Kylie hurried along beside Jon. As they entered the area to catch the elevator, they saw that it was just closing.

They rushed in, only to find that Calvin had gotten there before them.

"Hey, guys! You did come out," he said with pleasure. "Though you were probably just out and about and happened to see the group. But we're okay, right?"

"Not okay. I thought you were great," Kylie told him.

Her answer brought a smile to his lips. Then he frowned, but it turned to a grin. "Hey, you don't seem to be old at all—heading home a little early, huh?"

"Long day," Jon said briefly.

Calvin frowned again. "Yeah. The guys were talking earlier, saying that if they were girls, they'd be heading home. You get anywhere with the case?"

"Solving this kind of thing is like a puzzle," Jon told him. "More pieces are falling into place, though."

"Well, good," Calvin said approvingly. "Glad a good old G-Man is here. Uh, sorry, not old. Never mind. You know what I mean."

"Hey, you're almost a kid," Kylie told him. "You're going home early."

Calvin sighed and adjusted his grip on his guitar case. "It may be

Halloween on Sunday, but I have a Monday deadline. We're playing again tomorrow, but I owe some modifications to a game Monday."

"Ah, work by day and by night," Jon said.

Calvin grinned and shook his head. "Nah, I'm lucky. I love music. And when I get a good game going, well, that makes me happy, too. So, my work is play. How many people get to say that?"

"Not many," Jon agreed. He looked at Kylie. "She's tired."

"Hey, you're tired, too," Kylie protested.

"I was thinking of a nightcap, but...well, we'll get home. Not home—but back to the Brim House. Then we'll decide if we're getting a second wind, huh?" Jon said.

Kylie wasn't sure what he was getting at, but she smiled. "Sure."

"My floor," Calvin said, smiling to them both as he started getting off the elevator. He paused then, his hand on the sliding doors so they wouldn't shut on him. "Really, please. Solve this thing. I want Brenda to keep that place. She's great. It will wind up being some rich guy's toy that he may or may not play with the way this is going. Anyway, goodnight."

Then, he was gone.

"I just want to see if he really goes home," Jon said quietly. "And have an out for us to leave again."

"To where?"

"Pub hopping, what else? It's almost Halloween. It's Saturday night...and we need to catch a werewolf clown."

Kylie nodded. "Do you know how many pubs and bars there are in Salem?" she asked. "And this guy is probably luring his victims to his house or an apartment or a hotel room."

"Exactly. No, Kylie, I don't expect to simply walk into a pub and catch him poisoning a drink. I do want to see who is picking up people at the bars, though—and let them know that *they've* been seen."

They returned to the car and headed out of the garage. Once again, Calvin wound up being right in front of them.

He drove straight to his parents' house. Kylie and Jon went into Brim House and watched from the window. Calvin came out with Woof-Woof, walked him, and then went back in.

Jon stayed to the side of the window, looking out.

"Aren't we being peeping Toms now?" she asked softly.

He nodded. "I see Mrs. Matheson and the girls. They're making jack-o'-lanterns at the dining room table. I don't see Mr. Matheson."

"That doesn't mean anything."

"True. Next door...I see upstairs. Ginger is at her dressing table. I think she's talking to someone. Maybe Kenny is on the bed? Then again, maybe she's talking to herself. Who knows?" He turned to her. "We'll hop a few bars in the tourist area only."

"As you wish," Kylie said.

As they drove, Jon called Ben. He wanted him to get another public announcement out to the local channels, warning visitors about the murders and asking single women to be extremely careful about accepting drinks from strangers.

Ben said it would be done.

And he was true to his word. The partiers were out. But on the TV at the bar at the Cauldron, Ben's public service announcement played. He and Kylie didn't stay long, and they didn't see even one single woman, nor any pairs, actually—people were out in small groups.

It was the same when they traveled to the next pubs. After that, Jon looked at her and smiled grimly. "Ready for bed?"

"Is that a real question or a pick-up line?" she teased.

"Both," he told her.

"Very ready."

"For which?"

"Both."

They returned to Brim House, and this time, when Jon stood by the side of the downstairs window to look out, their neighboring houses were dark.

Jon swore softly.

"What?"

"The Daily place has a garage. There's no way to tell if Calvin went back out or not."

"Jon—"

"It's okay. We're going to get some sleep. Tomorrow will be...longer."

They headed upstairs. Kylie thought again that she'd crash into bed and it would be up to Jon to induce her to stay awake, but the shower once again beckoned her.

She headed that way, and he laughed.

"Remember last night?" he asked.

"Yep. Don't hog all the room," she told him.

He joined her and did an excellent job of convincing her to stay awake just a little bit longer.

But then, curled at his side, she slept. She thought that she would sleep deeply—she was so tired. The last days had been very long, and they had added some last-minute physical exertion into it all, so sleep should have come easily.

And it did. Sweet sleep, wonderful sleep, the kind that renewed the world.

Except it didn't last.

Darkness, the sweetness of rest, became a soft, swirling mist, growing brighter and brighter.

Kylie was in a kitchen. A small one. The kind in some of the hotels, usually referred to as a suite in those extended stay type places.

A blender sat on a counter, and Kylie saw her hands as she picked it up—only they weren't her hands. They were far larger, rougher, more bronzed. The nails were cut short, neat and masculine. Something trailed over the hands…little bits of fabric from what appeared to be an elegant shirt, perhaps something from a different age. But the hands…

Masculine. Beyond a doubt.

She was seeing through the eyes of a man.

She poured the mixed berry contents into two glasses and then added liberal portions of whiskey to each.

Strange. Her being fought her entrance into the man's mind. It made no sense. She was now entering into people in social situations, and she didn't want to be here…especially not in a man's body, while he was on a…a date? A hookup?

Dread already filled her. No, this was no simple date.

He smiled. She knew, though, of course, she couldn't see her face. She could feel what he was feeling.

Excitement, adrenaline rushing. This was planned. There would be a finale to make him proud and feel that he was godlike. That he had the power and was doing things that were just and right in the grand scheme of time and the universe.

No…

There was something of Kylie in this strange state. And she fought being there. He needed to seduce the woman—or what?

He called out to someone waiting on a sofa in a parlor/bedroom area.

"I'm so glad we left the bar. Much quieter. Much better here."

"I know," a woman replied. "I wasn't even going to come out tonight. The town is so wild right now, and with everything that's been going on…well, I'm glad that I met you with a friend."

"First trip, right?" he asked. He was still busy with his hands, reaching for something…a little container. He emptied the contents into one of the glasses.

"But you have friends in town?" he called.

What had he put in the drink? An aid for a sexual conquest?

Or something far worse?

Kylie wondered what she was doing here. Seeing through his eyes, feeling his strange emotions?

"My family lived here decades ago. I'm one of five kids," the woman said. "Between us…we have several friends still here, some just online, and others I see in Boston from time to time…which turned out to be great because we were introduced. Thankfully. I'd have walked around a bit, had that one drink at the bar, and headed back to my lonely room. I mean, we've been warned to be careful in the city."

"Thankfully, we were introduced. And in case you don't know, you're gorgeous."

"You're kind of pretty yourself."

"Ah, it's just the costume. But, thanks. All vampires are sexy, right?"

"Bela Lugosi in the classic *Dracula*?" the woman asked. "Not so much."

"But then came Franco Nero, for one. And *Fright Night*. Christopher Guest in the original—total charmer, or so it appeared."

"You love old movies?"

"You bet."

"Hey! Curious here. What color is your real hair?" the woman asked teasingly.

"Who said I had hair?"

They both laughed.

"Do you? Doesn't matter to me. My friend said that you were a great guy."

"I am a great guy."

He headed out of the kitchen. Through his eyes, *as* him, Kylie saw that the woman on the sofa was about thirty and dressed as a fairy, all in pastels with delicate wings that kept her from sitting back. She didn't seem to mind. Her hair was a soft blond color, and her eyes were an angelic blue, making the fairy costume a perfect fit for her.

He handed her one of the glasses.

The one into which he had emptied the contents of the strange little container while in the kitchen.

No. No, no, no, no, no!

This was a different experience. Different from…

She wasn't the victim.

She was a killer! And the two murdered tourists had been killed with strychnine, added to alcoholic drinks.

She saw the man's hand she currently inhabited. Saw the fringe of what she now knew to be a vampire costume.

Clown, werewolf, vampire. Hell, it was Halloween.

She had to take control. She needed to do something. Somehow, she had to overpower this man's mind and will. She was inside his head.

Control the hand. Control the hand…

The woman reached for the glass. He lifted his to her. "To Salem!" he said. "To those who created the great and amazing place that is Salem, Massachusetts. To all those in the past who brought us here together tonight."

The glass moved to the woman's lips.

Kylie found her strength of will within his mind.

She felt as if she were lifting a mountain.

But she did it. He suddenly screamed, "No!" And his hand reached out—knocking the glass out of the woman's hand.

She jumped, startled, and naturally mystified.

"Sorry, sorry!" the man said quickly. "I saw a bug—I—I didn't want you drinking a bug. It's all right. I'll just make another one."

But the woman was up, smiling but obviously a little thrown.

"I actually have an early-morning meeting with some other friends," she told him. "We promised each other breakfast for Halloween. I'm going to head back to the hotel. It was wonderful meeting you. Maybe tomorrow night we can get together again. But now…"

She was already at the door, a beautiful fairy in flight.

"I am so sorry."

"I'll see you tomorrow," she called cheerfully.

"You promise?" he asked. She paused at the door. He walked over to her, a grin in place as he lifted her chin and almost brushed her lips with a kiss.

"Tomorrow night. We'll start over," she whispered.

"I can't wait," he said huskily.

Kylie couldn't control his words or his actions. She had used all her strength to knock the glass from the woman's hand.

"I won't be a luscious fairy," she warned him.

"And I won't be a vampire. But I'll still find you."

"Promise?" she said teasingly, returning his word.

"Promise," he vowed. "I'll find you—at our bar."

She was out the door. He started to go after her and then swore vociferously as he fell flat. Kylie had managed to instill herself again and willed his feet to stay glued to the floor. The inner battle going on between them caused him to trip over his own two feet.

The woman was gone into the night.

And the mist in Kylie's dream or mind began to rise in the strange world that wasn't a dream but came to Kylie in her dreams. She felt warmth, tenderness, and the sensation of being held in strong arms...

"Kylie, Kylie!"

It was Jon. Of course. He held her, seemed to be trying to wake her, clearly afraid of where her strange mental nocturnal journeys might have taken her.

But she wasn't shaking. She wasn't afraid. She looked into true and bright eyes with hers.

"I—I was the killer, Jon. I saw through his eyes. I was in his home, and I was with him as he tried to poison his next victim."

"Another woman is dead?"

She shook her head, shaken but also incredibly relieved and amazed.

"Jon. I won! We battled in his mind. I controlled his hand and knocked away the glass with the poison."

Chapter 10

Jon studied Kylie's face, amazed at her incredible ability. He did not doubt that what she said was true.

"Okay," he said softly. "Where were you? And could you give a sketch artist any concept of the man or the woman he tried to seduce—and kill?"

"A hotel, a suite hotel. Or, you know, the kind that has those little kitchenettes," Kylie said. "I know I was a vampire, and the woman was a fairy. She looked to be about thirty, very pretty. Blond. And they made arrangements to see each other tomorrow night, both laughing and saying they'd be dressed differently. Jon, she just left him. She's out on the streets somewhere. If we could find her…"

He had his phone out, dialing Ben.

"Hey!" Ben said gruffly. "Don't you people ever sleep?"

"We need to find a really pretty fairy," Jon said quickly. "A blond—"

"You have a wife, Jon."

"Ben! The killer was just with her. He hesitated. He's staying at a hotel with a kitchenette."

"How the hell do you know this?" he demanded.

"Ben, just trust me. Insider tip. Can we get some men out on the streets looking for this woman?" He took a deep breath. "You know me, Ben. We need to find her. I'll hand you to Kylie. She can give you a better description."

He passed his wife the phone. She carefully described the woman and then noted Ben's number to put into her phone in case she remembered anything else later. When she was done speaking with Ben, she handed Jon's cell back to him.

"We're heading out ourselves. The woman wasn't staying at the hotel. It was where the man took her. Hanging up now. Ben, please, believe me."

He ended the call.

Kylie was already getting dressed. He threw on his clothing, and they rushed downstairs together.

"We need to find her," Jon said. "Kylie, you saved her life."

Kylie appeared to be almost pained. "Jon, I think I did. But…it was so hard! Harder than any physical effort I've ever made before. I'm astonished that it even worked. But if we don't stop him from seeing her again, he will kill her."

"Yes, he will," Jon agreed. "Werewolf, clown, vampire. No telling what he will be tomorrow and tomorrow night."

He paused at the car, looking down the block. The houses were dark. It was closing in on midnight—a family with kids wouldn't be out, older people usually went to bed fairly early, and Ginger did not seem the type to party late. Naturally, the block was quiet.

He was still suspicious. But Kylie had said that the man had the woman in a hotel room.

Anyone can rent a hotel room.

He called Ben back again. "Ben, is there any way to find out what hotels have rented to locals?"

"What?"

"You need an I.D. to get a hotel room. Can we find out if any hotels have rented rooms to locals?"

Ben sighed deeply. "I can start trying. But do you know how many people run bed and breakfast establishments or use those travel sites—"

"This is a hotel. A regular hotel."

"Jon, how do you—?"

"Please, Ben."

"All right, all right. I'm on the street myself. Looking for a fairy. At Halloween."

"Stop any fairy you see. We can sort them all out later."

Jon glanced at Kylie. She was watching the road intently. After they drove the streets in the tourist section, he expanded the search. But after forty-five minutes, he knew that the fairy would most probably be back in her hotel room.

With a sigh, he headed back to Brim House.

He had barely parked the car before he heard a cry of anguish.

Hopping out, he saw that Kenny Innes was lying in the yard, looking around desperately. "Help! Someone, please help. Ginger, oh my God. He has Ginger!"

Seeing Jon, Kenny tried to rise and fell again. Jon strode over to him. "Kenny?"

The man seemed to be hysterical with fear, and he was raving.

"He came back. He was back! Maybe he knew you were gone, but Ginger stepped out because she said a cat was crying on the porch or something, and I saw her with someone and hurried out. He slammed me with some kind of a giant hook and then…she was gone. I saw him going the same way he did before, dragging her. Please, help me. He's going to kill Ginger because…he wanted to kill you or her or…oh, God, I don't know! He's going to kill Ginger. He headed into the woods."

Kylie was behind him, reaching into her purse for her phone to call Ben. "Go!" she yelled. "Go!"

Jon headed toward the woods, wondering if the killer had known that Kylie had been in his mind.

He ran…

And almost ran through Obadiah Jones, standing there in the woods as if he knew that Jon would come.

* * * *

Jon hadn't even disappeared into the darkness before Kenny reached out for her, pleading, "Please, just help me to my feet. We need to call the police, if you'll just help me!"

Kylie hurried over to him, reaching down.

She wasn't sure what alerted her.

The hand.

She had seen the hand in detail in her vision from the hotel. For a few minutes, it had been her hand.

She started to back away, but he suddenly had her, clutching her wrist with a grip like steel, coming to his feet and swinging her to the ground. He reached into his pocket and produced a vial.

She was down, twisted at a funny angle.

But he didn't see that her cell phone was still in her left hand.

She was right-handed, and she wasn't sure what she could accomplish, but Jon was number 1 on her speed dial, and she could try…

"Drink!" he commanded, ripping the plug off the vial with his teeth.

"Drink!" he demanded. "I will get this down your throat. You…you…there is something about you, and I'm damned sorry. You're not right for this, but you have to die—what?"

He'd seen her phone.

She threw it out onto the grass, hoping it had dialed through.

That Jon was listening.

"You're creepy!" he screamed at her. "Drink this!"

He tried to force the vial to her lips. Strychnine. And she wasn't seeing this through other eyes this time.

It was happening to her.

But Kenny was accustomed to seducing and tricking vulnerable females. She wasn't helpless. She *was* terrified, of course.

But she knew that she had to act.

She had taken a few excellent self-defense classes since she and Jon had gotten married.

Kenny thought he had her, but he wasn't watching his balance—or his person. She smiled eerily, and when he frowned, confused, she shot up and raised a knee to his groin, causing him to scream in anguish, and allowing her a moment's freedom. She righted herself, ready to let out a scream that would wake the very dead before she kicked him in the head to make sure he'd stay down until Jon got back.

But sound never left her.

A woman came running out of the house, brandishing a gun.

It wasn't Ginger Radisson.

It was Mandy Nichols.

"What the hell are you doing, Kenny? This should have been over with already. We've got to get her out of here before that idiot comes back saying he's sorry he couldn't find Ginger."

"Idiot? I'm sorry, Jon *can* be an idiot at times, but not about his job. And if he comes back and doesn't find me, don't you think he'll know damned well that you're guilty?" Kylie asked.

"Not me," Mandy said. "I don't even live here. He won't find me. I'm just here because Kenny got beat up by a girl."

"Kenny has killed two women. At your suggestion, I'd guess?" Kylie said.

"You made me do it, Mandy. I loved you!" Kenny cried. "I did it all for you. This place, Ginger…I did it for you!"

He was still curled up in a fetal position. Obviously, Kylie had hurt him.

"Kenny likes killing. I just want the house back," Mandy said.

"What?" Kylie said incredulously.

Where the hell is Jon?

Mandy started to laugh. "Kenny likes women, but he gets a real hard-on when he gets to kill someone. As I said, I only want the house back. And, hey, growing up, I heard the coolest stories about my family, so it only seemed just that I point out the right people for Kenny to kill. Man, talk about dysfunctional! Mary kills Teresa, Teresa's kid kills Mary, Ezekiel goes to the gallows. What's more just than killing off a few of Teresa's great-great-a-million-times-greats or whatever grandkids? And stick a body in Brim House. I figured Brenda would run like a bat out of hell!"

"What? Why the hell didn't you just buy it yourself when it went up for sale?"

Mandy waved a hand in the air. "I got rid of those out-of-town buyers with no sweat whatsoever. Then the owner insisted he sell to Brenda. She had integrity, and she was such a good person, and she was paying his price. Blah, blah, blah. Enough. Kenny, give me the damned vial. I'll get the poison down her. By the way, how was it getting beat up by a girl? You look like you're really in pain. Oh, you are. Poor baby."

Mandy Nichols waved the gun at Kylie.

"Get in the house! Now. Or I'll put a bullet right between your eyes."

"Where is Ginger?" Kylie demanded. "And if you're going to put a bullet between my eyes, you'd better know where Ginger—and her phone is."

"Wasn't that a nice touch? Kenny and Ginger being so helpful, showing you the clown?" Mandy asked. "Ginger is knocked out, big dose of a sedative. We'll get to her later."

"Jon knows it's you," Kylie said.

"Bull! You didn't know it was me."

"I knew that Kenny did the actual killing," Kylie said. She looked at Kenny. "You see, I was in his mind. I was. He messed up tonight."

That startled Mandy enough that she forgot for a minute that she was holding the gun. Kylie started for her, but she quickly remembered.

"Bull. And get in here. I'll shoot your kneecap if you don't move. I'll put you in all kinds of pain—"

"Poison can be pretty painful from what I hear," Kylie said. "And it's not bull. Ask Kenny. I was in his head. I made him knock the drink out of that woman's hand, and then I made him trip and fall."

"She did," Kenny whispered, writhing on the ground. "Somehow, she gets into your head!" he cried.

Can I get back? Kylie wondered. She'd never tried to enter another human being—it had just happened.

If she couldn't really do it, could she psych him out?

She forced herself to smile at Mandy despite the terrifying concept of the gun pointed straight at her head.

"I can make Kenny get up and force that poison down your throat," she told Mandy and stared at Kenny. "Get the vial, Kenny. Do it!"

"Bull!"

She would never know if Kenny thought she was commanding him again or not. He started to get to his knees and crawl, and Mandy turned the gun on him.

She never fired. Jon leapt up onto the porch behind her and slammed her down to the wood.

Her gun went flying.

"You bastard!" Mandy raged. "You bastard! I need that house. A few lousy people died. Who cares? They were bitches anyway. Get off me. Get off me, get *off* me! You can't prove this. You can't prove anything. I'll beat you in court, I'll say you attacked Kenny and me, so convinced that you had it figured out in your self-righteous mind. I'll—"

Jon had cuffs in his pocket. While Mandy was still down, he used them on her, drawing her wrists to the small of her back.

He didn't wrench her to her feet. He left her cursing him and threatening all kinds of lawsuits as he hurried down the porch steps to Kylie, drawing her into his arms and looking into her eyes.

"I was there," he whispered. "I ran into Obadiah, but...Kylie, I knew. I knew when you called to me. I came around the back. Obadiah saw them both, and I didn't want to take any chances. I couldn't let her see that I was here. Kylie..."

She put a finger to his lips. "I'm okay," she told him. "I'm always okay. Because of you."

A police car came jerking up onto the grass.

Ben Miller stepped out. "The realtor?" he said incredulously.

"Yeah."

"He's lying! He's telling a terrible lie! That man over there called me saying he needed my help to get his girlfriend to sell the house," Mandy called from the ground. "And this idiot—"

"He called you at this hour of the night?" Ben asked. He looked at Kylie. "But Kenny Innes is the killer?" he asked.

"Yes, but she was pulling the strings. He must have had one hell of a crush on her. He lived with Ginger to be next door to Brim House. And he must have drugged her when he needed to slip out to commit the crimes," Kylie said. She noted that Obadiah Jones was coming down the steps. She looked at him, hoping that he saw the depth of her appreciation in her eyes.

He nodded to her and mouthed the words, "*Proud of you.*"

"No! He's a killer! I just came here to help," Mandy raged. "Anything they say is a lie!"

Jon pulled his phone out of his pocket and looked at it. He smiled. "Well, I'm guessing everything Mandy has had to say is...the truth? I think it will work in court, anyway."

"What?" Mandy screamed. She surged to her feet and stumbled down the steps, staring at Jon and then at Kenny, who was still curled on the ground.

"Idiot!" she raged at Kenny. "You let her call him?"

She went to kick him. But Kenny let out a scream of anguish unlike anything Kylie had ever heard. He locked a leg around hers, knocking her down, still handcuffed, to the ground.

Before anyone could stop him, he rolled over with the vial in his hands.

"Drink!" he cried, forcing the vial to her lips, even as Jon and Ben dove for the pair, desperate to separate them.

Epilogue

Ginger Radisson spent the night in the hospital, but she would be fine. When she could talk later in the day—Halloween—she kept crying. She'd had no idea. But then, she hadn't known why she felt like she was half-asleep all the time either.

Now, she knew.

And she would forever question her taste in men.

They were able to get Mandy Nichols to the hospital in time to save her life.

It seemed to be a consensus that everyone wanted her to stand trial—and to rot in jail for the rest of her life.

Kenny seemed to have lost his mind completely, but he would stand trial for his crimes, as well. It turned out that Mandy believed she had a family connection to Teresa Johnson's children, and therefore, felt it was fitting that those who had come later down the family tree pay and create insanity at *Haunted Happenings*—and at Brim House.

Brenda discovered that she had a few girlfriends who needed a place to live.

She wouldn't have to live in the infamous *haunted* house alone.

And she was keeping it.

Halloween was the holiday, but Monday was the day they celebrated. Calvin Daily insisted on having a goodbye appreciation dinner at his house, and the Matheson family, Mr. and Mrs. Flannery, and even Ned Olsen came over. They welcomed Brenda home and thanked Jon, Kylie, and Ben.

Everyone knew that Kenny insisted that Kylie was a real witch that could get into his head.

The good thing, of course, was that no one believed him.

They'd be driving back to Krewe headquarters in the morning, and Kylie would be back at the museum. Jon would return to doing whatever it was the Krewe called upon him to do with his exceptional knowledge and expertise.

For now, they stood in the front of the Daily house, looking back at Brim House before walking over to settle in for their last night.

Kylie leaned against Jon as he slipped his arms around her.

"You did it," he told her.

"I did some research. You knew all along that it was one of the neighbors."

"I suspected. The Mandy Nichols part...in the end, it made sense. She did have a key."

"Right."

He was quiet for a minute, and then he said softly, "Kylie, what you have is really something extraordinary. I believe that we are all gifted, all the Krewe members and friends. But what you have...you seriously saved that woman's life. But I worry about you so much. It's a tough burden, too. I love you, and I wish that I could take some of it off your shoulders. Make it all right."

She turned in his arms and looked up at him.

"Jon. Don't you know? I'm fine. I'm always fine. As long as I'm with you. And no matter what the future brings, I'll still be fine. Again, as long as I'm with you."

He pulled her closer. "I will always be with you," he said softly. "Always."

He let out a sigh and placed a damp and teasing kiss below her ear.

"Hey, want to make love in a haunted house one last time?"

She smiled.

Brim House was just a house. The ghosts they knew were friends. Like Obadiah.

Who never—ever—went into anyone's bedroom.

She broke from his arms and started across the street.

"Kylie?" he called.

She turned and laughed. "What the hell are you waiting for?" she teased.

But he wasn't waiting. He tore after her, sweeping her up in his arms.

And they headed into the house.

Because any place, anytime, anywhere was fine.

As long as she was with him.

* * * *

Also from 1001 Dark Nights and Heather Graham, discover The Dead Heat of Summer, Blood Night, Haunted Be the Holidays, Hallow Be The Haunt, Crimson Twilight, When Irish Eyes Are Haunting, All Hallows Eve, and Blood on the Bayou.

Sign up for the 1001 Dark Nights Newsletter
and be entered to win a Tiffany Key necklace.

There's a contest every month!

Go to www.1001DarkNights.com to subscribe.

**As a bonus, all subscribers can download
FIVE FREE exclusive books!**

Discover 1001 Dark Nights Collection Eight

DRAGON REVEALED by Donna Grant
A Dragon Kings Novella

CAPTURED IN INK by Carrie Ann Ryan
A Montgomery Ink: Boulder Novella

SECURING JANE by Susan Stoker
A SEAL of Protection: Legacy Series Novella

WILD WIND by Kristen Ashley
A Chaos Novella

DARE TO TEASE by Carly Phillips
A Dare Nation Novella

VAMPIRE by Rebecca Zanetti
A Dark Protectors/Rebels Novella

MAFIA KING by Rachel Van Dyken
A Mafia Royals Novella

THE GRAVEDIGGER'S SON by Darynda Jones
A Charley Davidson Novella

FINALE by Skye Warren
A North Security Novella

MEMORIES OF YOU by J. Kenner
A Stark Securities Novella

SLAYED BY DARKNESS by Alexandra Ivy
A Guardians of Eternity Novella

TREASURED by Lexi Blake
A Masters and Mercenaries Novella

THE DAREDEVIL by Dylan Allen
A Rivers Wilde Novella

BOND OF DESTINY by Larissa Ione
A Demonica Novella

THE CLOSE-UP by Kennedy Ryan
A Hollywood Renaissance Novella

MORE THAN POSSESS YOU by Shayla Black
A More Than Words Novella

HAUNTED HOUSE by Heather Graham
A Krewe of Hunters Novella

MAN FOR ME by Laurelin Paige
A Man In Charge Novella

THE RHYTHM METHOD by Kylie Scott
A Stage Dive Novella

JONAH BENNETT by Tijan
A Bennett Mafia Novella

CHANGE WITH ME by Kristen Proby
A With Me In Seattle Novella

THE DARKEST DESTINY by Gena Showalter
A Lords of the Underworld Novella

Also from Blue Box Press

THE LAST TIARA by M.J. Rose

THE CROWN OF GILDED BONES by Jennifer L. Armentrout
A Blood and Ash Novel

THE MISSING SISTER by Lucinda Riley

THE END OF FOREVER by Steve Berry and M.J. Rose
A Cassiopeia Vitt Adventure

THE STEAL by C. W. Gortner and M.J. Rose

CHASING SERENITY by Kristen Ashley
A River Rain Novel

A SHADOW IN THE EMBER by Jennifer L. Armentrout
A Flesh and Fire Novel

Discover More Heather Graham

The Dead Heat of Summer: A Krewe of Hunters Novella

Casey Nicholson has always been a little bit sensitive, and she puts it to use in her shop in Jackson Square, where she reads tarot cards and tea leaves. She's not a medium, but she *can* read people well.

When the ghost of Lena Marceau comes to her in the cemetery, shedding tears and begging for help, Casey's at first terrified and then determined. Lena knows she was the victim of a malicious murder. Assumes her husband was, as well, and now fears that her daughter and sister are also in danger. And all over what she believes is someone's quest to control Marceau Industries, the company left to Lena's late husband.

Casey isn't sure how she can help Lena. She isn't an investigator or with any arm of law enforcement. But when she receives a visit from a tall, dark and very handsome stranger—ironically an FBI agent—she realizes that she's being drawn into a deadly game where she must discover the truth or possibly die trying.

Special Agent Ryder McKinley of the Krewe of Hunters has his own strange connection to the case. Hoping to solve the mystery of his cousin's death, he arrives at Casey's shop during his hunt for answers and finds something wholly unexpected. He fears that Casey's involvement puts her in danger, yet she's already knee-deep in deadly waters. Unfortunately, there's nothing to do but follow the leads and hope they don't also fall prey to the vicious and very human evil hunting his family.

* * * *

Blood Night: A Krewe of Hunters Novella

Any member of the Krewe of Hunters is accustomed to the strange. And to conversing now and then with the dead.

For Andre Rousseau and Cheyenne Donegal, an encounter with the deceased in a cemetery is certainly nothing new.

But this year, Halloween is taking them across the pond—unofficially.

Their experiences in life haven't prepared them for what's to come.

Cheyenne's distant cousin and dear friend Emily Donegal has called from London. Murder has come to her neighborhood, with bodies just outside Highgate Cemetery, drained of blood.

The last victim was found at Emily's doorstep, and evidence seems to be arising not just against her fiancé, Eric, but against Emily, too. But Emily isn't just afraid of the law—many in the great city are beginning to believe that the historic Vampire of Highgate is making himself known, aided and abetted by adherents. Some are even angry and frightened enough to believe they should take matters into their own hands.

Andre and Cheyenne know they're in for serious trouble when they arrive, and they soon come to realize that the trouble might be deadly not just for Emily and Eric, but for themselves as well.

There's help to be found in the beautiful and historic old cemetery.

And as All Hallows Eve looms, they'll be in a race against time, seeking the truth before the infamous vampire has a chance to strike again.

* * * *

Haunted Be the Holidays: A Krewe of Hunters Novella

When you're looking for the victim of a mysterious murder in a theater, there is nothing like calling on a dead diva for help! Krewe members must find the victim if they're to discover the identity of a murderer at large, one more than willing to kill the performers when he doesn't like the show.

It's Halloween at the Global Tower Theatre, a fantastic and historic theater owned by Adam Harrison and run by spouses of Krewe members. During a special performance, a strange actor makes an appearance in the middle of the show, warning of dire events if his murder is not solved before another holiday rolls around.

Dakota McCoy and Brodie McFadden dive into the mystery. Both have a. special talent for dealing with ghosts, but this one is proving elusive. With the help of Brodie's diva mother and his ever-patient father—who were killed together when a stage chandelier fell upon them—Dakota and Brodie set out to solve the case.

If they can't solve the murder quickly, there will be no Thanksgiving for the Krewe...

* * * *

Hallow Be the Haunt: A Krewe of Hunters Novella

Years ago, Jake Mallory fell in love all over again with Ashley Donegal—while he and the Krewe were investigating a murder that replicated a horrible Civil War death at her family's Donegal Plantation.

Now, Ashley and Jake are back—planning for their wedding, which will take place the following month at Donegal Plantation, her beautiful old antebellum home.

But Halloween is approaching and Ashley is haunted by a ghost warning her of deaths about to come in the city of New Orleans, deaths caused by the same murderer who stole the life of the beautiful ghost haunting her dreams night after night.

At first, Jake is afraid that returning home has simply awakened some of the fear of the past...

But as Ashley's nightmares continue, a body count begins to accrue in the city...

And it's suddenly a race to stop a killer before Hallow's Eve comes to a crashing end, with dozens more lives at stake, not to mention heart, soul, and life for Jake and Ashley themselves.

* * * *

Crimson Twilight: A Krewe of Hunters Novella

It's a happy time for Sloan Trent and Jane Everett. What could be happier than the event of their wedding? Their Krewe friends will all be there and the event will take place in a medieval castle transported brick by brick to the New England coast. Everyone is festive and thrilled... until the priest turns up dead just hours before the nuptials. Jane and Sloan must find the truth behind the man and the murder--the secrets of the living and the dead--before they find themselves bound for eternity--not in wedded bliss but in the darkness of an historical wrong and their own brutal deaths.

* * * *

When Irish Eyes Are Haunting: A Krewe of Hunters Novella

Devin Lyle and Craig Rockwell are back, this time to a haunted castle in Ireland where a banshee may have gone wild—or maybe there's a much more rational explanation—one that involves a disgruntled heir, murder, and mayhem, all with that sexy light touch Heather Graham has turned into her trademark style.

* * * *

All Hallows Eve: A Krewe of Hunters Novella

Salem was a place near and dear to Jenny Duffy and Samuel Hall -- it was where they'd met on a strange and sinister case. They never dreamed that they'd be called back. That history could repeat itself in a most macabre and terrifying fashion. But, then again, it was Salem at Halloween. Seasoned Krewe members, they still find themselves facing the unspeakable horrors in a desperate race to save each other-and perhaps even their very souls.

* * * *

Blood on the Bayou: A Cafferty & Quinn Novella

It's winter and a chill has settled over the area near New Orleans, finding a stream of blood, a tourist follows it to a dead man, face down in the bayou.

The man has been done in by a vicious beating, so violent that his skull has been crushed in.

It's barely a day before a second victim is found... once again so badly thrashed that the water runs red. The city becomes riddled with fear.

An old family friend comes to Danni Cafferty, telling her that he's terrified, he's certain that he's received a message from the Blood Bayou killer--It's your turn to pay, blood on the bayou.

Cafferty and Quinn quickly become involved, and--as they all begin to realize that a gruesome local history is being repeated--they find themselves in a fight to save not just a friend, but, perhaps, their very own lives.

About Heather Graham

New York Times and *USA Today* bestselling author, Heather Graham, majored in theater arts at the University of South Florida. After a stint of several years in dinner theater, back-up vocals, and bartending, she stayed home after the birth of her third child and began to write. Her first book was with Dell, and since then, she has written over two hundred novels and novellas including category, suspense, historical romance, vampire fiction, time travel, occult and Christmas family fare.

She is pleased to have been published in approximately twenty-five languages. She has written over 200 novels and has 60 million books in print. She has been honored with awards from booksellers and writers' organizations for excellence in her work, and she is also proud to be a recipient of the Silver Bullet Award from the International Thriller Writers and was also awarded the prestigious Thriller Master in 2016. She is also a recipient of the Lifetime Achievement Award from RWA. Heather has had books selected for the Doubleday Book Club and the Literary Guild, and has been quoted, interviewed, or featured in such publications as The Nation, Redbook, Mystery Book Club, People and USA Today and appeared on many newscasts including Today, Entertainment Tonight and local television.

Heather loves travel and anything that has to do with the water and is a certified scuba diver. She also loves ballroom dancing. Each year she hosts a ball or dinner theater raising money for the Pediatric Aids Society and in 2006 she hosted the first Writers for New Orleans Workshop to benefit the stricken Gulf Region. She is also the founder of "The Slush Pile Players," presenting something that's "almost like entertainment" for various conferences and benefits. Married since high school graduation and the mother of five, her greatest love in life remains her family, but she also believes her career has been an incredible gift, and she is grateful every day to be doing something that she loves so very much for a living.

Discover 1001 Dark Nights

COLLECTION ONE
FOREVER WICKED by Shayla Black ~ CRIMSON TWILIGHT by Heather Graham ~ CAPTURED IN SURRENDER by Liliana Hart ~ SILENT BITE: A SCANGUARDS WEDDING by Tina Folsom ~ DUNGEON GAMES by Lexi Blake ~ AZAGOTH by Larissa Ione ~ NEED YOU NOW by Lisa Renee Jones ~ SHOW ME, BABY by Cherise Sinclair~ ROPED IN by Lorelei James ~ TEMPTED BY MIDNIGHT by Lara Adrian ~ THE FLAME by Christopher Rice ~ CARESS OF DARKNESS by Julie Kenner

COLLECTION TWO
WICKED WOLF by Carrie Ann Ryan ~ WHEN IRISH EYES ARE HAUNTING by Heather Graham ~ EASY WITH YOU by Kristen Proby ~ MASTER OF FREEDOM by Cherise Sinclair ~ CARESS OF PLEASURE by Julie Kenner ~ ADORED by Lexi Blake ~ HADES by Larissa Ione ~ RAVAGED by Elisabeth Naughton ~ DREAM OF YOU by Jennifer L. Armentrout ~ STRIPPED DOWN by Lorelei James ~ RAGE/KILLIAN by Alexandra Ivy/Laura Wright ~ DRAGON KING by Donna Grant ~ PURE WICKED by Shayla Black ~ HARD AS STEEL by Laura Kaye ~ STROKE OF MIDNIGHT by Lara Adrian ~ ALL HALLOWS EVE by Heather Graham ~ KISS THE FLAME by Christopher Rice~ DARING HER LOVE by Melissa Foster ~ TEASED by Rebecca Zanetti ~ THE PROMISE OF SURRENDER by Liliana Hart

COLLECTION THREE
HIDDEN INK by Carrie Ann Ryan ~ BLOOD ON THE BAYOU by Heather Graham ~ SEARCHING FOR MINE by Jennifer Probst ~ DANCE OF DESIRE by Christopher Rice ~ ROUGH RHYTHM by Tessa Bailey ~ DEVOTED by Lexi Blake ~ Z by Larissa Ione ~ FALLING UNDER YOU by Laurelin Paige ~ EASY FOR KEEPS by Kristen Proby ~ UNCHAINED by Elisabeth Naughton ~ HARD TO SERVE by Laura Kaye ~ DRAGON FEVER by Donna Grant ~ KAYDEN/SIMON by Alexandra Ivy/Laura Wright ~ STRUNG UP by Lorelei James ~ MIDNIGHT UNTAMED by Lara Adrian ~ TRICKED by Rebecca Zanetti ~ DIRTY WICKED by Shayla Black ~ THE ONLY ONE by Lauren Blakely ~ SWEET SURRENDER by Liliana Hart

COLLECTION FOUR

ROCK CHICK REAWAKENING by Kristen Ashley ~ ADORING INK by Carrie Ann Ryan ~ SWEET RIVALRY by K. Bromberg ~ SHADE'S LADY by Joanna Wylde ~ RAZR by Larissa Ione ~ ARRANGED by Lexi Blake ~ TANGLED by Rebecca Zanetti ~ HOLD ME by J. Kenner ~ SOMEHOW, SOME WAY by Jennifer Probst ~ TOO CLOSE TO CALL by Tessa Bailey ~ HUNTED by Elisabeth Naughton ~ EYES ON YOU by Laura Kaye ~ BLADE by Alexandra Ivy/Laura Wright ~ DRAGON BURN by Donna Grant ~ TRIPPED OUT by Lorelei James ~ STUD FINDER by Lauren Blakely ~ MIDNIGHT UNLEASHED by Lara Adrian ~ HALLOW BE THE HAUNT by Heather Graham ~ DIRTY FILTHY FIX by Laurelin Paige ~ THE BED MATE by Kendall Ryan ~ NIGHT GAMES by CD Reiss ~ NO RESERVATIONS by Kristen Proby ~ DAWN OF SURRENDER by Liliana Hart

COLLECTION FIVE

BLAZE ERUPTING by Rebecca Zanetti ~ ROUGH RIDE by Kristen Ashley ~ HAWKYN by Larissa Ione ~ RIDE DIRTY by Laura Kaye ~ ROME'S CHANCE by Joanna Wylde ~ THE MARRIAGE ARRANGEMENT by Jennifer Probst ~ SURRENDER by Elisabeth Naughton ~ INKED NIGHTS by Carrie Ann Ryan ~ ENVY by Rachel Van Dyken ~ PROTECTED by Lexi Blake ~ THE PRINCE by Jennifer L. Armentrout ~ PLEASE ME by J. Kenner ~ WOUND TIGHT by Lorelei James ~ STRONG by Kylie Scott ~ DRAGON NIGHT by Donna Grant ~ TEMPTING BROOKE by Kristen Proby ~ HAUNTED BE THE HOLIDAYS by Heather Graham ~ CONTROL by K. Bromberg ~ HUNKY HEARTBREAKER by Kendall Ryan ~ THE DARKEST CAPTIVE by Gena Showalter

COLLECTION SIX

DRAGON CLAIMED by Donna Grant ~ ASHES TO INK by Carrie Ann Ryan ~ ENSNARED by Elisabeth Naughton ~ EVERMORE by Corinne Michaels ~ VENGEANCE by Rebecca Zanetti ~ ELI'S TRIUMPH by Joanna Wylde ~ CIPHER by Larissa Ione ~ RESCUING MACIE by Susan Stoker ~ ENCHANTED by Lexi Blake ~ TAKE THE BRIDE by Carly Phillips ~ INDULGE ME by J. Kenner ~ THE KING by Jennifer L. Armentrout ~ QUIET MAN by Kristen Ashley ~

ABANDON by Rachel Van Dyken ~ THE OPEN DOOR by Laurelin Paige ~ CLOSER by Kylie Scott ~ SOMETHING JUST LIKE THIS by Jennifer Probst ~ BLOOD NIGHT by Heather Graham ~ TWIST OF FATE by Jill Shalvis ~ MORE THAN PLEASURE YOU by Shayla Black ~ WONDER WITH ME by Kristen Proby ~ THE DARKEST ASSASSIN by Gena Showalter

COLLECTION SEVEN
THE BISHOP by Skye Warren ~ TAKEN WITH YOU by Carrie Ann Ryan ~ DRAGON LOST by Donna Grant ~ SEXY LOVE by Carly Phillips ~ PROVOKE by Rachel Van Dyken ~ RAFE by Sawyer Bennett ~ THE NAUGHTY PRINCESS by Claire Contreras ~ THE GRAVEYARD SHIFT by Darynda Jones ~ CHARMED by Lexi Blake ~ SACRIFICE OF DARKNESS by Alexandra Ivy ~ THE QUEEN by Jen Armentrout ~ BEGIN AGAIN by Jennifer Probst ~ VIXEN by Rebecca Zanetti ~ SLASH by Laurelin Paige ~ THE DEAD HEAT OF SUMMER by Heather Graham ~ WILD FIRE by Kristen Ashley ~ MORE THAN PROTECT YOU by Shayla Black ~ LOVE SONG by Kylie Scott ~ CHERISH ME by J. Kenner ~ SHINE WITH ME by Kristen Proby

Discover Blue Box Press
TAME ME by J. Kenner ~ TEMPT ME by J. Kenner ~ DAMIEN by J. Kenner ~ TEASE ME by J. Kenner ~ REAPER by Larissa Ione ~ THE SURRENDER GATE by Christopher Rice ~ SERVICING THE TARGET by Cherise Sinclair ~ THE LAKE OF LEARNING by Steve Berry and M.J. Rose ~ THE MUSEUM OF MYSTERIES by Steve Berry and M.J. Rose ~ TEASE ME by J. Kenner ~ FROM BLOOD AND ASH by Jennifer L. Armentrout ~ QUEEN MOVE by Kennedy Ryan ~ THE HOUSE OF LONG AGO by Steve Berry and M.J. Rose ~ THE BUTTERFLY ROOM by Lucinda Riley ~ A KINGDOM OF FLESH AND FIRE by Jennifer L. Armentrout

On Behalf of 1001 Dark Nights,

Liz Berry, M.J. Rose, and Jillian Stein would like to thank ~

Steve Berry
Doug Scofield
Benjamin Stein
Kim Guidroz
Social Butterfly PR
Ashley Wells
Asha Hossain
Chris Graham
Chelle Olson
Kasi Alexander
Jessica Johns
Dylan Stockton
Kate Boggs
Richard Blake
and Simon Lipskar

Made in the USA
Coppell, TX
13 October 2021

63993178R00073